I HEARD THE CRACK OF THE BAT.

The ball was coming right toward me.

It was mesmerizing. I was hypnotized.

I couldn't move. I *wanted* to move, but I guess those cells in my central nervous system didn't fire. In the few milliseconds it took for the ball to reach me, my eyes didn't have time to tell my brain to DUCK! Or GET OUT OF THE WAY! BAIL! DIVE! GET YOUR GLOVE UP! DO SOMETHING!

And then the ball hit me.

It sounded like a bomb going off in my head.

Everything went dark.

The last thing I remember was hearing somebody yell, "Call 911!"

Also by Dan Gutman

The Get Rich Quick Club
Johnny Hangtime
Casey Back at Bat

Baseball Card Adventures:

Honus & Me
Jackie & Me
Babe & Me
Shoeless Joe & Me
Mickey & Me
Abner & Me
Satch & Me
Jim & Me
Roberto & Me

My Weird School Daze:

Mrs. Dole Is Out of Control!
Mr. Sunny Is Funny!
Mr. Granite Is from Another Planet!
Coach Hyatt Is a Riot!
Officer Spence Makes No Sense!
Mrs. Jafee Is Daffy!
Dr. Brad Has Gone Mad!
Miss Laney Is Zany!
Mrs. Lizzy Is Dizzy!
Miss Mary Is Scary!
Mr. Tony Is Full of Baloney!
Ms. Leakey Is Freaky!

My Weird School:

Miss Daisy Is Crazy!
Mr. Klutz Is Nuts!
Mrs. Roopy Is Loopy!
Ms. Hannah Is Bananas!
Miss Small Is off the Wall!
Mr. Hynde Is Out of His Mind!
Mrs. Cooney Is Loony!
Ms. LaGrange Is Strange!
Miss Lazar Is Bizarre!
Mr. Docker Is off His Rocker!
Mrs. Kormel Is Not Normal!
Ms. Todd Is Odd!
Mrs. Patty Is Batty!
Miss Holly Is Too Jolly!
Mr. Macky Is Wacky!
Ms. Coco Is Loco!
Miss Suki Is Kooky!
Mrs. Yonkers Is Bonkers!
Dr. Carbles Is Losing His Marbles!
Mr. Louie Is Screwy!
Ms. Krup Cracks Me Up!

Ray & Me

A Baseball Card Adventure

Dan Gutman

HARPER
An Imprint of HarperCollins*Publishers*

Ray & Me

 For information address HarperCollins Children's Books, a division of HarperCollins Publishers, 10 East 53rd Street, New York, NY 10022.
www.harpercollinschildrens.com

Library of Congress Cataloging-in-Publication Data
Gutman, Dan.
Ray & me : a baseball card adventure / Dan Gutman. — 1st ed.
p. cm.
Summary: After recovering from being hit in the head during a baseball game, Stosh travels back in time to try to save Ray Chapman, a batter who was killed by a pitch in New York in 1920.
ISBN 978-0-06-123483-5
1. Chapman, Ray, d. 1920—Juvenile fiction. 2. Mays, Carl, 1891—Juvenile fiction. [1. Chapman, Ray, d. 1920—Fiction. 2. Mays, Carl, 1891—Fiction. 3. Baseball—Fiction. 4. Time travel—Fiction.] I. Title. II. Title: Ray and me.
PZ7.G9846Ray 2009 2008019645
[Fic]—dc22 CIP
AC

Typography by Alison Klapthor
11 12 13 14 15 CG/CW 10 9 8 7 6 5 4 3 2
❖
First paperback edition, 2011

To Sweet Adeline Berlin

Acknowledgments

I would be helpless without Bill Francis, Pat Kelly, and Andrew Newman of the National Baseball Hall of Fame; Dave Kelly of the Library of Congress; Drs. Dan Cho and Stephen Dante; Mike Sowell; Nina Wallace; Tom Lalicki; and J. J. Fennell. Thanks to all.

I knew that the sight of his silent form would haunt me as long as I live.

—Carl Mays

Introduction

With a baseball card in my hand, I am the most powerful person in the world. With a card in my hand, I can do something the president of the United States can't do, the most intelligent genius on the planet can't do, the best athlete in the universe can't do.

I can travel through time.

—Joe Stoshack

Ray & Me

1

Wally Pipp and Me

I FELT SICK. ALL MORNING, I FELT LIKE I WAS GOING TO throw up. It must've been something I ate. As much as I love baseball, I really didn't feel like playing today.

"Hey, Stosh, c'mere! I need to talk to you 'bout somethin'."

It was my coach, Flip Valentini. He always calls me Stosh. Most people do. Flip is a really old guy, and he's a member of the Baseball Hall of Fame, so I do what he says. I dragged my tired body off the bench and went over to where he was standing near the backstop.

The rest of the team was straggling in to Dunn Field on their bikes. Kids were tying their shoelaces and stretching. The sound of baseballs popping into gloves was starting to echo across the grass. Louisville can get pretty hot by the end of April. It felt like it was already 90 degrees.

"I need to talk to you too, Flip," I said.

The coach put an arm around my shoulder. I supported some of his weight. He's been like a father to me ever since my parents split up.

Flip wasn't *always* a Hall of Famer. What happened was that I took him back in time with me, to 1942. When we got there, Flip was a teenager. We met the great pitcher Satchel Paige, and Satch taught him how to throw his famous Hesitation Pitch. After that, some nut tried to kill us; and I was forced to leave Flip in 1942. Long story short, Flip got to live his adult life all over again in the past; and when I got back to the present day, he was inducted into the Baseball Hall of Fame.

Time travel is funny that way. You never know what's going to happen when you start messing around with history. But that's a story for another day.

I was all ready to tell Flip I didn't feel well enough to play, but he didn't give me the chance.

"Stosh," he said, "Billy Hoobler's mom called me an hour ago. His uncle died suddenly, and they gotta go to Texas for the funeral."

I felt bad for Billy. He is a good pitcher and a good guy. I met his uncle once. He came to one of our practices and showed us the right way to slide.

"Who's gonna take Billy's place?" I asked Flip.

"You are," Flip told me. "I need you to pitch today."

WHAT?

Me? Pitch? I'm a shortstop. I've always played short.

"I—I can't pitch, Flip," I sputtered. "Why can't Johnny or Zack pitch?"

"'Cause Johnny and Zack can't hit the broad side of a barn," Flip whispered so they wouldn't hear. "I need somebody who can get the ball over the plate."

"Oh, man," I complained. "I feel like crap today, Flip. I'd probably give up ten runs."

"Stosh, ya know who we're playin' today?" Flip asked.

I looked across the diamond. It said SHIMOJIMA on the other team's uniforms. That's the name of an optician in town.

"Those bums can't hit their way out of a paper bag," Flip told me. "They only have one good hitter, that kid Cameron Considine. You can pitch around him."

"I have a headache, Flip," I whined.

"Oh, I know a foolproof cure for headaches," Flip told me.

"What is it?"

"Pitch two innings and call me in the morning," Flip said. "Come on, Stosh, I'm beggin' ya! You got a good arm. Just give me two innings. Six lousy outs. Tell you what. If you pitch, I'll take you and your mom out for ice cream after the game."

"I really didn't want to play today at all," I told Flip. "Can't I sit this one out?"

"Sit this one out? Sit this one *out*?" Flip shook his head and raised his voice. "Did I ever tell you the story of Wally Pipp?"

"Here we go again!" Somebody behind me chuckled.

Flip is always telling us stories about the good old days of baseball. For an old guy, he has incredible recall. Flip can't remember where he left his glasses, but he can remember who was the on-deck batter when Bobby Thomson hit his "Shot Heard 'Round the World" in 1951.

(It was Willie Mays, by the way.)

Everybody gathered around: Colin Creedon, Luke Lee, Matt Connelly, Ryan Riskin, Dylan Wilson, Sean-Patrick Racaniello, and the other guys on our team. With a name like Wally Pipp, you'd think that at least *one* of us would have heard of him.

"Wally Pipp was a great first baseman," Flip told us. "Played for the Yanks in the 1920s. Led the league in homers. Twice. Anyways, Pipp got a lotta headaches ever since he got creamed in a hockey game as a kid. Then one day in 1925, he asked for a couple of aspirins 'cause he had a splittin' headache, and the manager said he could take the day off."

"So?" I asked. It sounded like a pretty lame story to me.

"Y'know who replaced Wally Pipp at first base that day?" Flip asked us.

"Who?" we all said.

"A 22-year-old kid," Flip said. "His name was Lou

Gehrig. Ever hear of *him*?"

"So Lou Gehrig got his shot because Wally Pipp had a headache?" Matt Connelly asked.

"That's right," Flip said. "And Gehrig was so good that he became the new first baseman. The Yankees sold Pipp to Cincinnati. So what's the moral to the story, boys?"

"You're gonna send Stosh to Cincinnati?" asked Ryan Riskin.

What a dork.

"Okay, okay," I said. "I'll pitch."

"Attaboy!" Flip said, clapping me on the back. He put a clean, white baseball in my glove.

2

Keep It Simple, Stupid

I WALKED OUT TO THE MOUND. OUR CATCHER, LUKE LEE, squatted behind the plate and gave me a target. I tossed in a couple of easy warm-up pitches, bouncing both of them in the dirt two feet in front of the plate. Flip was right about one thing. My headache was gone. I had other things to worry about now.

It's weird throwing off a pitcher's mound. You're so *high*. I tried to get comfortable up there. Each warm-up pitch came a little closer to the strike zone.

I glanced to my right. The kids on the other team were leaning against the backstop, checking me out and whispering to each other. I looked off to the bleachers on my left until I found my mom in the third row. She was easy to spot because she was wearing her white nurse's uniform. She must have just gotten off work.

Mom gave me the thumbs-up. My dad was nowhere

to be seen. He makes it a point not to be around if my mom is there. And vice versa. They don't exactly get along.

I pumped in a few more warm-up pitches to Luke. The umpire took a swig from his water bottle and brushed off the plate with a whisk broom.

"You ready, son?" he asked me.

"Ready as I'll ever be," I replied.

"Let's get this party started. Play ball!"

Luke trotted out to the mound and dropped the ball in my glove.

"Okay, Stosh," Luke said. "You know the KISS signs?"

"KISS signs?" I asked. "What are you talking about?"

"KISS. Keep It Simple, Stupid," Luke said. "If I put down one finger, it means you throw the fastball, okay? Two fingers, you throw the curve."

"I don't have a curve," I told Luke.

"I got news for you," he replied. "You don't have a fastball either. Just try to hit my mitt, okay? We'll get you through this."

Luke was right. I've got a decent arm, and I can throw accurately; but my hands are small. I don't throw that hard. *What was I doing out here?* I asked myself. I glanced over at Flip. He just nodded to me.

Luke went back behind the plate. Everybody got into position. The first batter dug a toe into the batter's box. I took a deep breath.

"You can do it, Stosh! . . . You're the man! . . . One-

two-three, baby! Just throw strikes! . . . No batter! . . . Let 'em hit it, Stosh! We'll cover you."

Infield chatter is so meaningless. I never noticed until people started yelling it at *me*.

I went into my windup and threw the first pitch as hard as I could. It sailed way over Luke's mitt and slammed into the backstop behind the batter's head. A few kids snickered. The batter stepped out and called time.

"Settle down, Stosh," Flip called out. "Nice and easy. Just throw strikes, babe."

I was trying too hard. I threw the next pitch much slower, and the kid actually swung and missed. He missed the next one too, and the umpire called the pitch after that a strike even though it was a few inches outside. The kid didn't complain.

"One out!" called the ump.

I turned around and threw a secret smirk at my infielders. Hey, I struck a guy out! Who says pitching is so hard?

The batter must have freaked out when I threw my first pitch so wild. *Hmmm,* I thought. Maybe I should chuck the first pitch to *every* batter behind his head. That would keep 'em on their toes.

Focus on the now, I told myself. One out. Nobody on. *If the ball comes to me,* I reminded myself, *throw it to first base.* Luke trotted out to talk to me again.

"You're doin' good," he told me. "That guy thought you were throwing change-ups. He kept waiting for the fast one."

"Yeah," I said. "Lucky he didn't know I don't *have* a fast one."

"It won't take the rest of 'em long to find out," Luke said. He pulled his mask down and trotted back behind the plate.

The next guy swung at my first pitch and hit a wicked shot right up the middle. I dove out of the way. Man, the ball comes at you a lot *faster* when you're on the pitcher's mound! You got to have quick reflexes.

The batter stopped at first base with a single, and the number three batter came up. He swung at my first pitch too, and hit an easy one-hopper right back to me. I gloved the ball cleanly, whirled around, and threw it to Dylan Wilson covering second. He stepped on the bag for the force play. I thought he might have had time to throw to first for a double play, but he decided not to risk it. That's okay.

"Smooth!" Flip said, clapping his hands. "Nice play, boys!"

One more and we'd be out of the inning. The cleanup batter was up. I had never met the kid, but I knew his name. Cameron Considine. Everybody calls him Hammerin' Cameron. He's only 13, just like the rest of us, but the guy looks like he's in high school. Nobody deserves to have muscles like that. Our outfielders moved back until they were standing right in front of the fence. Luke came out to the mound to chat again.

"This guy hits the ball *hard*," he told me. "Let's

walk him. We'll get the next guy easy, and that'll be the third out."

"Oh, come on," I told Luke. "That'll put the runner into scoring position. Besides, intentional walks are lame."

Luke sighed. "Just don't give him anything good to hit, okay?" he instructed. "Make him swing at a bad pitch. If he lays off, he'll walk and we'll get the next guy."

"Sounds like a plan," I said.

I took a good look at Hammerin' Cameron as he tapped the dirt off his cleats with his bat. He had rolled up the sleeves of his uniform to show off his muscles. Probably a jerk, I figured.

Hammerin' Cameron didn't look so tough. I was starting to feel a little cocky, I guess. You know—the bigger they come, the harder they fall. I decided to see what would happen if I threw him a strike. So I grooved my first pitch right down the middle of the plate.

Cameron just looked at it.

Strike one. Ha! Everybody is so afraid of this kid, they don't challenge him. He never expected me to throw him a strike.

So I threw him another one. Right down Broadway.

"Strike two!" called the umpire.

Ha! Just as I thought. Hammerin' Cameron was a big wus.

"You got 'im now, Stosh!" somebody hollered. "One more!"

"Protect the plate, Cameron!" yelled somebody from the other side.

Luke came running out to the mound for another conference. I wished he would just stay behind the plate and catch. I was on a roll. He was throwing off my rhythm.

"What are you, crazy?" Luke said to me. "Do *not* throw another pitch over the plate! This guy will hit it into the next county!"

"Okay, okay," I assured Luke. "I was just messing with his mind."

Luke went back and set up a target with his mitt a foot off the outside corner. He wanted to make Cameron go fishing for the next one. Gee, don't be *too* obvious!

Cameron pumped his bat across the plate and glared at me. He was P.O.'d now. I went into my windup and aimed for Luke's mitt.

I missed it. I don't know what happened. The ball sailed inside. It was going right over the plate.

Cameron swung at it.

I heard the crack of the bat.

The ball was coming right toward me.

It was mesmerizing. I was hypnotized.

I couldn't move. I *wanted* to move, but I guess those cells in my central nervous system didn't fire. In the few milliseconds it took for the ball to reach me, my eyes didn't have time to tell my brain to DUCK! Or GET OUT OF THE WAY! BAIL! DIVE! GET YOUR GLOVE UP! DO SOMETHING!

And then the ball hit me.

It sounded like a bomb going off in my head.

Everything went dark.

The last thing I remember was hearing somebody yell, "Call 911!"

3

Two Weeks Later . . .

THE FIRST THING I NOTICED WHEN I WOKE UP WAS THAT MY *shoulder* was killing me.

I opened my eyes. I was in a hospital room. All kinds of machines were hooked up to me, gently beeping. What was even more surprising was that right next to my bed were my mom and dad. They were asleep, Dad sitting in his wheelchair and Mom sitting next to him, her head on his shoulder.

Whoa! Did I travel through time, back to the days when my folks were still married? Or maybe I died and this was heaven. But why would there be a hospital in heaven? And why would a tube be sticking out of my nose? The top of my head felt funny. I touched it. I was bald! There were bandages up there.

Suddenly, Mom's eyes fluttered open.

"Joey!" she shrieked, jumping to her feet. Dad

woke up with a start. Soon they both were hugging me and laughing and crying all at the same time. They were acting like I had been kidnapped or something and they were seeing me for the first time in years.

"Did we win the game?" I asked.

"The game?" my mother said, laughing and grabbing a tissue. "Nobody cares about *that*! The game was canceled."

"That was two weeks ago, Butch," my dad added.

Two weeks? It felt like two minutes ago.

"What have I been doing for the last two weeks?" I asked.

"Not a whole lot," Dad said.

"Joey," said my mom, "you've been in a coma."

What?! Wow! No wonder I was in the hospital. No wonder my mom and dad were sitting there next to each other. No wonder they freaked out when I woke up. And no wonder I was so *hungry*.

"Butch, you could have died," my dad said.

The first thought that crossed my mind was that it was worth almost dying to see my parents together again. They were actually holding hands!

I tried to remember what happened. Somebody was shouting, "Call 911! Call 911!" Then the memories started flooding back into my brain.

Flip asked me to pitch. I didn't want to because I was feeling lousy. He told me the story about that guy Wally Pipp who had a headache. I agreed to pitch, and I was doing pretty well until that kid Hammerin' Cameron came up. That was the last thing I remembered.

"The ball hit you in the head, Joey," my mom said, stroking my hand. "The doctor said it might have been traveling at a hundred miles per hour."

"You fell on your shoulder and hurt that too," my dad told me. "It was dislocated, but the doctors were able to pop it back into place."

For a moment, I had forgotten about my shoulder. Once Dad reminded me, it hurt again.

"The boy who hit the ball, Cameron Considine, was so upset," Mom told me. "We were *all* upset. You were lying there on the ground, not moving. Cameron thought he killed you. He had to go into counseling."

This was all too much to absorb at once. Before this, I had never been seriously injured in my whole life. The worst thing that ever happened to me was that time in third grade when I ran into a tree chasing a Frisbee. But I never broke a bone. Never had to go to the emergency room. Never even had any stitches.

On the table next to my bed was a stack of articles that had been clipped from magazines and newspapers.

LOUISVILLE BOY IN COMA AFTER BASEBALL ACCIDENT

LOUISVILLE, KY. May 2 —Thirteen-year-old Joe Stoshack remains comatose three days after getting hit in the head by a batted ball during a game at Dunn Field. The youngster, who had never pitched before, has not responded

"You're famous, Butch!" my dad said.

I was reading the article about myself when a doctor walked into the room. He was a tall African-American man, and he had a big smile on his face.

"Doctor, he woke up!" my mother exclaimed.

"I can see that!" the doctor said. "Like I told you; your son's head is as hard as a rock! So this is the famous Joseph Stoshack, eh? It's a pleasure to meet you awake."

The doctor shook my hand and told me his name was Louis Wright. He said he was a Yankees fan, like my dad.

"Am I gonna be okay?" I asked him.

"I'm not sure," he replied. "Did you ever hear about the time Dizzy Dean got hit in the head by a ball?"

"No," I admitted.

"Dean was not exactly the smartest guy in the world," Dr. Wright told me. "So after he was released from the hospital and it was clear that he wasn't seriously hurt, one newspaper ran the headline: X-RAYS OF DEAN'S HEAD REVEAL NOTHING."

The doctor threw back his head and laughed. We all did.

"Dr. Wright may have saved your life, Joey," my mother said. "He's one of the most respected brain surgeons in the country."

"Did you operate on my brain?" I asked.

"No," the doctor said. "We treated you with medication to reduce the swelling of your brain. And we put a pressure monitor on your skull to make sure we *didn't* have to operate on your brain. We did stick a probe into your skull, though. That's why we had to shave your head."

"Oh, man, I must look like a real dork!"

"Joey!" Mom said. "You're lucky to be *alive*!"

"Your mother is right," Dr. Wright told me. "In more severe brain injury cases where the brain swells, we have to remove part of the skull to relieve the pressure. Even then the patient doesn't always survive."

I didn't want to think about that. But I was grateful that I was in good hands.

"Sorry," I said.

"Your mom was the real hero," said Dr. Wright. "She knew exactly what to do. She made sure you weren't gagging or choking or had your tongue blocking an airway to prevent you from breathing. Then she elevated your head and kept it stable in case there was a spinal injury. And of course, she got you to the hospital as quickly as possible."

"Any nurse knows to do that," Mom said modestly.

"But not all of them think of it in a crisis," Dr. Wright said, "especially with their own child. Now, Joseph, I want to try a few simple tests to make sure your brain is functioning properly."

"Are you going to stick more electrodes into my skull?" I asked.

"No, I just need to ask you a few questions. Let's say you're playing third base. There are runners on first and second. One out. The batter smacks a grounder to third. What do you do?"

"That's easy," I said. "I glove the ball and step on third to force out the lead runner. If there's time, I throw to second for the double play."

"Why not go for a triple play?" the doctor asked.

"You said there was one out before the ball was hit," I told him. "There *can't* be a triple play."

"Very sharp," Dr. Wright said. "What if you're playing second base? Runner on first. One out. Grounder to your right."

"I scoop it up and flip the ball to the shortstop covering second," I told him. "He throws to first to complete the double play."

"Good," Dr. Wright said. "Now tell me this. Why is

it quicker to run from first base to second than it is to run from second base to third?"

He had me there. The distance between the bases is identical, of course. There was no reason why it should take longer or shorter to run between any two bases.

"Uh, I don't know," I admitted.

"Because there's a short stop in the middle," the doctor said, throwing back his head with laughter. "Get it? Short stop?"

I got it. It was the oldest baseball joke in the book. How could I forget it?

"You'll be out of here in no time," said Dr. Wright.

"Will I be a hundred percent normal again?" I asked.

"Yes, but do us all one favor, Joe."

"What?" I asked.

"Stick with shortstop," he said. "You make a lousy pitcher."

4

The Best Pitcher I Never Heard of

I FELT LIKE I WAS ALL BETTER, BUT DR. WRIGHT INSISTED that I stay in the hospital for a few days so he could keep an eye on me. It was hard to sleep in that bed, and the food was terrible; but at least I had some visitors. A bunch of the guys on my team crowded into the room and had a great time making fun of my bald head. Instead of a get well card, they gave me the ball that hit me. Everybody signed it too. Nice!

Just before visiting hours were over, the kid who hit the ball, Cameron Considine, showed up. He came with his parents. Cameron was all remorseful and apologetic, but I told him to forget about it. He didn't mean to hit me. Accidents happen in sports.

I'm not sure I convinced him that it wasn't his fault. He was still quiet and kept his head down when he left.

There was nothing good on TV, so I started looking through those articles my mom had clipped from the newspapers. It turns out I wasn't the only pitcher to get hurt by a batted ball. In 2005, near Chicago, a kid named Bill Kalant was pitching, and he got hit in the head by a line drive. He was in a coma for two weeks, just like me. In 2006, a 12-year-old New Jersey boy named Steven Domalewski got hit in the chest with a ball, and it stopped his heart for a while. Domalewski lived; but his brain was damaged, and he's paralyzed.

In 2003, a pitcher in Montana named Brandon Patch *died* after getting hit in the head by a batted ball. The same thing happened in 2007 to a minor-league first base coach in Arkansas. In fact, between 1991 and 2001, 17 baseball players were killed by batted balls. So I was lucky.

What happened to these other guys apparently had sparked a big discussion about metal baseball bats. Back in the old days, bats were only made out of wood, of course. Aluminum and other metal bats started showing up in the 1970s. They don't break as easily as wood bats, and they have a bigger sweet spot. They're also lighter, so you can swing them faster. And if you swing a bat faster, you can hit the ball harder. Everybody knows that.

Because of what happened to kids like me, some leagues have switched back to wooden bats. In 2007, North Dakota banned metal bats at high school games entirely.

I was reading about all this stuff when I noticed somebody standing at the door. I looked up and saw my coach, Flip Valentini. He had his hat in one hand and a pint of Ben & Jerry's ice cream in the other. Chunky Monkey.

"I promised you I'd get you ice cream if you pitched . . ." Flip began. He put his hat down on a chair, and then he started to cry.

It was a little weird. I'm not used to grown-ups crying, especially guys like Flip. I didn't know how to react. I guess Flip took what happened to me harder than anyone. He pulled out a handkerchief and wiped his eyes. It took him a while to calm down and ask me how I was feeling.

"Not bad," I said, "but my shoulder is sore, and I can't sleep in this bed. Last night I had a dream that I was hit in the head with a pitch, and then I woke up in the hospital. It was weird."

"After what you been through, it sounds normal to me," Flip said.

"How's the team doing?" I asked him.

"Fuhgetaboutit. We stink without you, Stosh."

"Ah, you're just saying that to make me feel better."

"It was my fault," Flip told me. "I shoulda listened when you said you didn't feel good. I shouldn't put any kid on the field unless he's a hundred percent."

"Hey, I should've caught that ball," I told him. "Then none of this would have happened."

Flip told me that I was putting my glove up when

the ball hit me. It was just coming at me too fast to react in time.

I told him about the metal bat controversy, but he knew all about it.

"If the kid hit that ball with wood, you woulda had a fraction of a second more to react," Flip said. "They gotta get rid of all this new stuff—designated hitters, fake grass, domed stadiums, and fake bats. That ain't baseball."

"The doctor told me if Cameron hit the ball an eighth of an inch up or down on the bat, I might have lost an eye," I told Flip.

"It's a game of inches," Flip said. "That's what I always say. If you lost an eye, I don't know what I woulda done. Stosh, you're like a son to me."

Flip wiped his eyes again.

"I'm gonna take some time off," I told him. "I mean, before I play ball again."

"Don't do that," Flip said, and then he stopped himself. "Ah, don't listen to me. Grown-ups ain't always right. Especially old fools like me. Do what you think is right."

I had to laugh. I wasn't sure if I should listen to Flip when he told me what to do or listen to him when he told me not to listen to him when he told me what to do.

"Anything you say, Flip," I said.

He reached into his jacket pocket and pulled out his wallet. I thought he was going to give me some money, but instead he took out a small baseball card.

103
CARL MAYS
PITCHER
NEW YORK "YANKEES" A. L.

"I wanna show you somethin'," he said, putting the card on my bed.

I didn't pick it up. I know what happens when I pick up a baseball card. In a few seconds, I get this tingling feeling in my fingertips. The feeling moves through my hand, up my arm, and over my whole body. The next thing I know, I'm in a different place and a different time period—the year on the card.

I leaned forward to look at the card. It looked really old. Because the word "Yankees" was in quotation marks, I figured that it must have been printed shortly after the Yankees got their name.

"Carl Mays," Flip said, after seeing the puzzled look on my face. "He played mostly with the Red Sox and the Yankees way back, almost a hundred years ago now."

"Never heard of him," I said.

"That's too bad," Flip told me. "He was a great pitcher. Good sinking fastball."

Flip opened up the ice cream and took two spoons out of his pocket so we could share. While we ate, he rattled off Carl Mays's numbers.

Carl Mays

The guy had a lifetime record of 208-126, so he won nearly twice as many games as he lost. And his ERA. was just 2.92. That's impressive. In 1921, he was 27-9 and led the American League in wins, winning percentage, games pitched, and innings pitched. He won 20 games in five seasons. He pitched 31 straight innings in the World Series without walking a batter. He pitched 30 complete games, in *two* seasons. One day, he won both games of a doubleheader.

Wow. Carl Mays was phenomenal. I thought I knew a lot about baseball history, but Flip has forgotten more than I'll ever know.

"Mays was a great hitter too," Flip added. "Hit .343 one year."

"Is he in the Hall of Fame?" I asked. He certainly had Hall of Fame statistics. But I thought I knew the names of all the Hall of Famers, and I'd never heard of Carl Mays.

"Nope," Flip replied.

"Why not?"

"There was this one little problem with Carl Mays," Flip said.

"What was that?" I asked.

"Well, one day in 1920, when he was with the Yankees, he killed a man."

5

The Ultimate Sacrifice

WOW. I KNEW THE YANKEE LINEUP IN THE 1920S WAS called "Murderers' Row." But I never knew that one of the Yanks actually *killed* somebody.

Flip lowered his voice to a whisper, like he was telling me a secret.

"Stosh, there've been more than 33 *million* pitches thrown in major-league history," Flip said. "I figured it out on a calculator. But only *one* of 'em ever killed a guy."

"Who was it?" I asked.

"He played for the Cleveland Indians," Flip told me. "His name was Ray Chapman. Chappie, they called him."

"I never heard of him either."

"Hardly anybody remembers him," Flip said. "It was August 16, 1920. The Yankees were playing Cleveland—"

The door suddenly opened and Doctor Wright came in. He was carrying a clipboard. Flip stopped in the middle of his sentence.

"It's okay," the doctor said. "I know all about Joseph's . . . gift."

"How do *you* know?" I asked.

I didn't like the idea of every Tom, Dick, and Harry knowing I could travel through time with baseball cards. People might think I was some kind of freak.

"Your mother told me," said Dr. Wright.

"What?!"

"Now, don't be mad at her, Joseph," he said. "As your doctor, it's important for me to know any abnormalities having to do with your brain functioning."

Dr. Wright told me that he didn't believe my mother at first. The idea of somebody traveling through time sounded crazy. And using a baseball card as a time machine? That's just nuts. Science fiction stuff.

"Your mother is pretty convincing," Dr. Wright said.

Then he turned to Flip and handed him the clipboard, looking a little embarrassed. I thought it had some important medical information on it, but the paper was blank.

"Mr. Valentini," Dr. Wright continued, "I heard you were visiting Joseph, and I wanted to meet you. I'm sure you hate this, but my son is ten years old and he'll be furious with me if I didn't ask you for your autograph."

"Fuhgetaboutit," Flip said as he took the pen and scrawled his name on the paper. "You a baseball fan, Doc?"

"Oh, a *big* fan!"

"Then pull up a chair," Flip told Dr. Wright. "You ever hear of a fella named Ray Chapman?"

"That guy on the Indians who died?" asked the doctor. "Sure. As a brain surgeon, I take special interest in cases like that."

Dr. Wright said he was supposed to be visiting other patients, but he could spare a few minutes. He brought a chair over to the side of my bed. I dug into the Chunky Monkey while Flip told the story.

"It was a real tight pennant race between the Yankees, the Indians, and the White Sox in 1920," Flip told us. "Cleveland was in first place, but just barely. It was August, so the season was almost over. The Yankees and the Indians were playing at the Polo Grounds in New York."

The Polo Grounds. I knew it like I know my name. I met the legendary Jim Thorpe at the Polo Grounds in 1913. But that's a story for another day.

"Wait a minute," Dr. Wright interrupted. "Why would the Yankees be playing at the Polo Grounds? That was where the New York Giants played, and they were in the National League. Why didn't the Yankees play at Yankee Stadium?"

"Yankee Stadium didn't open until 1923," Flip said.

"Aha. Go on."

"Mays was a submarine sinker baller," Flip said. "He threw underhand and *hard*. I saw him pitch when I was a little kid. They used to call him Sub."

"Was he wild?" I asked. "Is that why he hit Chapman?"

"Nah," Flip said. "Just the opposite. Mays had great control. Hardly ever walked anybody. But he hit a lot of guys. He had a reputation as a beanballer. A headhunter."

"Was he trying to hit Chapman on purpose?" asked Dr. Wright.

"I don't think so," Flip told us. "The Indians had a three-run lead. Chapman led off the fifth inning. The third pitch from Mays was way inside. Chapman didn't try to get out of the way. He never moved. Bang, right in the left temple."

I touched my left temple. It was exactly where the ball hit me.

"No batting helmet?" I asked.

"Not in 1920," Flip said.

"That would do it," said Dr. Wright. "A fastball could very easily fracture a man's skull. Do you know if they performed an operation on Chapman?"

"I dunno," Flip said. "But he didn't make it through the night. He died at the hospital."

"What they knew about head trauma was very

limited in 1920," Dr. Wright told us. "If something like that happened today, the patient almost certainly would live."

Flip nodded. "Ray Chapman died, and Mays—well, part of him died too. For the rest of his life, nobody cared about his pitching. People only knew him for one thing—throwing the pitch that killed a guy. It kept him out of the Hall of Fame, if you ask me."

"Was Ray Chapman any good?" I asked.

"Oh, yeah!" Flip said. "Chappie coulda been a Hall of Famer himself. "Flashy shortstop. He could turn the double play. Not a lot of power, but he hit over .300 three times. And fast? He just exploded out of the batter's box. Stole 52 bases one year. In 1918, he led the American League in runs scored and walks. Great bunter too. He led the league in sacrifices three times."

"It could be said that he made the *ultimate* sacrifice," said Dr. Wright.

"You could say that," Flip said. "Cleveland won the game by that one run."

"Talk about taking one for the team," Dr. Wright said sadly.

"Ray Chapman was 29 when he died," Flip said. "He was in his prime."

"What a sad story," Dr. Wright said, shaking his head. "That one pitch ended a man's life and ruined the life of another man. One pitch. One little mistake. If the ball had hit him anywhere but the

Ray Chapman

temple, I'm sure he would have lived."

"Like I say," Flip said, "it's a game of inches."

"How do you know so much about those guys, Flip?" I asked. "You weren't there that day, were you?"

"Nah, I was too little," said Flip. "I got interested in Carl Mays and Ray Chapman when I moved to Kentucky. It turns out that both of 'em were born right here. They grew up south of Louisville about 150 miles apart. Both of 'em were even born in the same year—1891."

I bolted up from the bed. An idea had popped into my mind. It was like in the cartoons when a lightbulb appears over somebody's head. I was so excited.

"I could go back in time!" I exclaimed. "I know exactly when and where it happened! I could stop it. It would be so easy. I could save Ray Chapman's life! I could get Mays and Chapman into the Hall of Fame—just like I helped you get into the Hall of Fame, Flip!"

"Whoa!" Dr. Wright said. "Slow down, Joseph. You've been in a coma. You're not going *anywhere*. You need to rest."

Dr. Wright picked up his clipboard, and Flip grabbed his hat.

"I'm sorry, Doctor," Flip said. "I never shoulda got him all riled up. I'm such an old fool."

"Not at all," Dr. Wright said. "The story was fascinating. Joseph, I'll check up on you later today."

They closed the door behind them. It was quiet in

my room. I could have turned on the TV or skimmed through a magazine, but I didn't feel like it. I was thinking about Ray Chapman and Carl Mays.

As I picked up the empty ice-cream carton to throw it in the trash, I noticed something. Flip had forgotten to take his Carl Mays baseball card. It was sitting there on the bed.

I touched the card lightly with my fingertips. I could do a little test, I thought. Nothing serious. I could zip back to 1920 for a minute, just to make sure I could still do it.

Dr. Wright had specifically told me to stay in my room and rest. But I don't particularly like being told what I can or can't do. Who does? Flip said it himself: grown-ups aren't always right.

I picked up the card and thought about Carl Mays and Ray Chapman. I could save a man's life. The lives of *two* men, really.

I thought about 1920. *The Polo Grounds. The Yankees. The Indians. The fifth inning.*

I waited. And waited. But nothing happened.

I must have been doing something wrong, I figured, because when I pick up a baseball card, I usually feel a buzzy, tingling sensation in my fingertips. It's sort of like the feeling you get when you brush your fingers against a TV screen. And then my whole body starts tingling. And then, after a few seconds, I disappear and reappear in the year on the baseball card.

I tried again, concentrating really hard on the

card. *August 1920. New York City. The Polo Grounds. Carl Mays. Ray Chapman. The fifth inning.*

Nothing.

My power was gone!

6

Home Games

When I got home from the hospital, I was in for another shock. As Mom drove up our street, every tree had a ribbon tied around it. So did some of the mailboxes. I asked my mother what was going on, and she said, "It's all for you."

A lot of people must have read those articles about me in the newspapers. In my room there was a mailbag full of letters telling me how brave I was and get well cards from all over the world. Some guy in Japan said he promised to quit smoking if I got better. People had dropped off cakes in the shape of baseball bats and home plates.

It's kind of weird that you have to almost die before nice stuff like this happens to you. I know if that ball had missed my head by an inch, nobody would have baked me a cake or told me how brave I was.

The welcome home was great. But even though I was in my own bed, I kept having bad dreams about getting hit by a ball. And I was really disturbed that I couldn't travel through time anymore. I had thought the power was part of me, that it was something I'd always have. I figured that as I grew older, maybe I would find a way to use my power not just to meet famous baseball players, but also to help the world in some way. Do some good for humanity.

But now I could forget about that idea. I should have done it while I had the chance.

When I was leaving the hospital, Dr. Wright had told me it didn't surprise him that I'd lost my power. The human brain is a very delicate instrument, he said. Any time it takes a heavy blow, there's a good chance the victim is going to lose some mental ability. He said that some people can't walk after a blow to the head. Some people have to learn how to talk all over again. Football players who get multiple concussions are sometimes handicapped for life.

"If traveling through time with baseball cards is the only brain function you've lost," Dr. Wright told me, "you're a very lucky young man."

Well, I didn't feel very lucky. I had to stay home for three weeks; and even though we get about 200 channels, there's nothing good on TV during the day. I was bored out of my mind. The worst part was that even though I couldn't go to school, I still had to keep up with my schoolwork. Every day, one of my friends dropped off a new package of homework for me.

Once my dislocated shoulder healed, Mom got me some new video games to help pass the time while she was at work. I spent a lot of that time organizing my baseball card collection too. Flip said I could keep the Carl Mays card as a present. I guess he still felt guilty about making me pitch when I wasn't feeling well.

The story that Flip told me about Carl Mays and Ray Chapman was one of those things I couldn't get out of my mind. While I was stuck at home and fooling around on the computer, I found myself googling Ray Chapman. I wanted to find out more about him. There was plenty of stuff online.

Like Flip said, Ray Chapman was hit on August 16, 1920. The thing I found most interesting was that there were no batting helmets in those days. This was hard to believe. Pitchers were throwing rock-hard baseballs 90 or so miles an hour to batters whose heads were just inches away from the strike zone. And all they wore on their heads was a cloth cap! It was only a matter of time before somebody got killed. How could they not know that? Why didn't they do anything about it?

If Ray Chapman had been wearing a batting helmet, it would have saved his life. The pitch would have glanced off the helmet. Chapman would have jogged to first, maybe with a little ringing in his ears. The game would have continued like it was no big

RAY CHAPMAN DIES; MAYS EXONERATED

Widow Brings Body of Ball Player, Killed by Pitched Ball, Back to Cleveland.

CITY MOURNS SHORTSTOP

Pitcher Who Threw Ball Unnerved by Accident — Other Teams Would Bar Him.

MIDNIGHT OPERATION FAILS

Player's Brain Crushed by Force of Blow — District Attorney Says Accident Was Unavoidable.

The body of Ray Chapman, the Cleveland shortstop, who died early yesterday in St. Lawrence Hospital after being hit in the head by a pitched ball thrown by Carl Mays at the Polo Grounds

deal. Everything would have been different. Today, Ray Chapman and Carl Mays would very possibly be in the Baseball Hall of Fame together.

Sometimes the smallest thing changes everything.

The only problem, of course, is that batting helmets didn't exist back in 1920. I didn't know if this was because it didn't occur to anybody to invent one or because they didn't have the technology in those days to make one.

I made up my mind. If my power ever came back to me, I would travel to 1920 with a batting helmet for Ray Chapman. This was a matter of life and death.

After a week at home, the bandages came off my head, and I started to look normal again. Two weeks later, I had some peach fuzz on my head. You couldn't see the little scar on my skull where Dr. Wright had inserted the pressure monitor. I was feeling stronger every day. I was itching to get back to school.

"I'm fine," I told my mother when three weeks were almost up.

"You're staying home," she said. "Doctor's orders."

We fought about it. There was a lot of yelling and stomping upstairs and slamming doors. But in the end, I did what she told me to do. She's my mom, after all. Once I'm 18, I guess I'll be able to make my own decisions.

In the meantime, I did something I didn't tell my mother about. Every day, after she left for work, I ran through my brain exercises. I would take an old baseball card and hold it in one hand. Then I would concentrate on it. I would focus on the card, on the player, and on the time period.

I figured that when we get a cut in our skin, the cut heals in a few days. If we break our leg, it heals. So my brain could heal too, right? I should be able to get my power back. Then I could go to 1920 and save Ray Chapman's life.

I didn't have a Ray Chapman card. But I realized that I didn't need one. I had the Carl Mays card. At the moment Chapman got hit in the head, I knew where Mays was—exactly 60 feet and 6 inches away, on the pitcher's mound. So if I could get to Mays, I could get to Chapman.

Well, nothing happened. The brain exercises didn't work. It was like a switch had been flipped and my power turned off. It was frustrating. I felt like my little "mental workouts" were a waste of time. I couldn't travel through time anymore, and that was it. I might as well get used to it and get on with my life.

But I kept at it, anyway. As soon as Mom pulled out of the driveway to go to work, I would pull down the shades in my room, take out my Carl Mays card, and sit on my bed. I'd close my eyes and think about where I wanted to go. I'd imagine myself in New York City in 1920. Running around the outfield grass at the Polo Grounds. Catching an imaginary fly ball. Sliding into second base.

And then, one day, just as I was about to give it all up, I felt the slightest tingling sensation in my fingertips.

I dropped the card.

I was so excited! There was so much to do. Quickly, I jumped up and ran around the house gathering the stuff I would need for my trip. There was a batting helmet in the garage. I took out some of the foam from the inside so it would be big enough to fit a grown man's head. Then I found a laundry bag to put the helmet in.

I rummaged around my desk drawer until I found an unopened pack of baseball cards. I would need it to get home again. You see, a baseball card is like a ticket to me. Just like an old card takes me back to the past, a new card brings me back to the present day.

I gathered my stuff next to me on the bed and shut my eyes. This was it. I picked up the card. Nothing happened at first. Nothing *ever* happens at first. It takes a while. But now I was hopeful.

I thought about Ray Chapman. No, no, that wouldn't do me any good. I thought about Carl Mays. It was *his* card. I had to get to him. In 1920. New York City.

After a minute or so, I started to feel a tingling sensation. It was very weak at first, but I could feel it coming on. It was like trying to start a campfire with a match and some twigs. If you do it right and the wind doesn't blow out the match, and you're lucky, it will ignite.

The tingles moved up my fingers and through my wrist. The fire was catching! My whole arm was vibrating, and then the feeling washed across my chest.

I had my power back!

I wanted to open my eyes and see it happen, but I didn't dare. My whole body was buzzing now, and I had reached the point of no return.

The fire was blazing. I felt myself disappear.

7

Sweet Adeline and the Great Houdini

I WAS FLOATING ON A CLOUD, AND MY ENTIRE BODY WAS made of thin glass. I could see right through myself. It felt so real. I had a bat in my hands, waiting for a pitch.

There was just one other person up there on the cloud with me. It was Hammerin' Cameron, and he was the pitcher. He went into a big, exaggerated, cartoony windup.

The pitch was coming right at me. I tried to back away, but I couldn't move. I was frozen in place, like a statue. The ball crashed into my head.

Millions of tiny pieces of me exploded off in all directions, reflecting sunlight in slow motion. I was hollow. There was nothing left of me.

When I opened my eyes, I realized it had been a nightmare. That never happened before. Hopefully, it would never happen again.

I looked around to see that I was surrounded by about a million people. But I wasn't home, and I wasn't at the Polo Grounds—or at any other ballpark. I was in the middle of a city street.

Why does this always happen to me? Why is it that I never end up where I *want* to be? Where I *need* to be? Just once, I wish it would be easy.

Whenever they show time travel in the movies or on TV, some guy just steps into a booth and twists a few knobs; and the next thing you know, he's sharing a cup of tea with Napoleon or George Washington or somebody like that. But with baseball cards, I discovered, you never know where you're gonna wind up. It's not fair.

People were pushing and shoving. It looked like I might be in the right town at least—New York City. I had been there before. Maybe this was Times Square on New Year's Eve, I thought. Nah, that couldn't be right. It was daytime, and it was too hot and muggy to be December.

I slipped the Carl Mays card into my pocket. Mays was probably somewhere in this crowd. But how would I find him? All the men looked the same, wearing those goofy, old-time straw hats.

Everybody was looking up in the air; and when I looked up, I saw one of the strangest sights I'd ever seen.

There was a guy dangling upside down high above the street. His ankles were tied together with thick rope, which extended up to a crane. His body

It was one of the strangest sights I had ever seen.

appeared to be wrapped in some kind of cloth too.

He was wriggling around like a worm up there, and people below were pointing and *ooh*ing and *ahh*ing. A gust of wind came along, and the guy hanging from the rope swayed one way, then the other. It looked like he was going to bang into the side of a building.

"Oooooooooh!" moaned the crowd.

There was a little girl standing near me. She looked about nine years old.

"Excuse me," I asked. "What's that guy doing up there?"

"Jeepers creepers!" the girl replied. "Didn'tja ever hear of the Great Houdini?"

Well, sure I'd heard of Houdini. He was probably the most famous magician ever. I just didn't know he would hang himself upside down in public.

Squinting into the sun, I could see that Houdini was struggling to get out of the cloth that was wrapped around him. I guessed it was a straitjacket, one of those things they used to put on crazy people so they couldn't escape.

Houdini was twisting and turning and grunting while the crowd below cheered him on. I couldn't take my eyes off him. Nobody could.

"He's nutty as a fruitcake," said one man.

"He's swell!" a lady said.

The performance, if you can call it that, went on for about 15 minutes. Gradually, Houdini managed to loosen the cloth that was binding him. He got one arm free, then the other. Finally, he extended his arms out to his sides dramatically and threw off the straitjacket. It fell to the street below.

The crowd exploded in cheers.

"Come see the Great Houdini perform his complete act at the Orpheum Theatre tonight at eight o'clock sharp!" hollered some guy with a megaphone. "The Great Houdini will do his famous Chinese Water Torture Cell Escape. No shackles can bind the Great Houdini! Tonight at eight o'clock sharp! The Orpheum Theatre."

The crowd let out another cheer; and then, quite suddenly, everybody started walking off in different directions. They were like roaches when you turn on the light. Within a minute, the crowd was gone and this looked like any other city street.

If Carl Mays was in that crowd, he was gone now too. I had blown my chance. I'd never find him in all the millions of people in New York City.

I thought about calling it quits and going home.

A newspaper was lying on a bench. I picked it up.

The New York Journal

NEW YORK, MONDAY, AUGUST 16, 1920.

Aha! Monday, August 16, 1920. That was the date Ray Chapman was killed. Well, at least I showed up on the right day.

The newspaper cost two cents, I noticed. It had only 24 pages, and it wasn't separated into different sections. I flipped through until I found the sports pages.

AMERICAN LEAGUE.

	Won.	Lost.
Cleveland	70	40
Chicago	72	42
New York	72	43
St. Louis	53	54
Boston	49	58
Washington	47	59
Detroit	41	67
Philadelphia	35	76

The Indians had a slim lead over the White Sox and Yankees.

The Indians were in first place—barely, just like Flip had said. Scanning down the page, I saw this:

BASEBALL TO-DAY, 3:30 P. M. POLO Grounds. Yankees vs. Cleveland.—Advt.

Judging by the angle of the sun in the sky, it was probably close to noon. Chapman was going to get hit in the fifth inning. That meant I had around four hours to save his life.

I was about to ask somebody how to get to the Polo Grounds, but something stopped me. Carl Mays *had* to be somewhere near me now. That was the way it always worked.

I looked around, trying to spot Mays. A man stepped out of an unmarked doorway about 25 feet away. I rushed over there, hoping to grab the door before it shut; but I was too late. The wooden door slammed in my face.

I knocked twice. A few seconds went by before a thin slot opened in the door at about eye level. I could hear music and noise inside.

"What's the password?" a man's voice asked gruffly.

"Password?" I said. "I don't know any password."

"Then whaddaya want?" All I could see were the man's eyes.

"I'm trying to find a guy," I said. "His name is—"

"Scram!" the voice said. "Put an egg in your shoe and beat it."

"But I—"

"Go play in the traffic, kid."

The slot in the door closed. I was about to turn away when it opened again. Another pair of eyes stared at me.

"Don't mind Louie," a woman's voice said with a giggle. "He's a flat tire. Did you bring the stuff?"

"What stuff?" I asked, but she had already closed the slot and opened the door.

She was pretty, with bright red lips, short wavy hair, and skinny eyebrows that looked like they were drawn on with a pencil. She was holding a rose in her hand. Behind her, there was a party going on. It looked like a nightclub. Happy people were dancing to jazz music. There was a live band playing. The scene looked like one of those old gangster movies my mom likes to watch.

"Hey, you're kinda cute!" the lady said. "Come on in!"

I hesitated. There was a lot of drinking going on in there, and I didn't want to get in trouble. On the other hand, Carl Mays might be in this place. And besides, it wasn't every day that a pretty girl told me I was cute. I stepped through the doorway.

"My name's Adeline," she said. "Y'know, like in

"You're kinda cute!' she said. "Come on in!"

the song 'Sweet Adeline'? You can call me Addie."

I'd never heard of the song before.

"Joe Stoshack," I said, shaking her hand. "You can call me Stosh."

"Stosh, I like that," she said. "Hey, what's with the odd threads? Where ya from, Stoshie?"

I looked down at my jeans and sneakers.

"I'm from . . . out of town," I said.

"Way out, looks like to me."

"Louisville, Kentucky," I said.

"That how they dress in Louisville?"

"Pretty much."

"C'mere, Stoshie!"

Addie grabbed my hand and pulled me past some couples who were dancing while swigging from bottles of whiskey. They didn't even bother with glasses. As she dragged me toward the bar, she told me that the password was Woodrow, same as the president's first name.

"Hey, Jimmy!" she yelled to a guy mixing drinks behind a bar. "Where's that zoot suit we had layin' around? I think it would fit my friend Stoshie."

"Get that ragamuffin outta here, Addie!" the bartender yelled back. "You want the cops to bust in and find a kid in here?"

"Ah, dry up, Jimmy, ya big sap!" Addie yelled at him. "Mind your potatoes."

"Says you, Addie!"

"Don't mind him," Addie whispered to me. "He's just steamed because we're gonna get the right to vote."

"Huh?"

"You ain't heard?" she said. "On Wednesday, Tennessee is gonna vote on women's suffrage, and word is it's gonna pass. They're gonna add an amendment to the Constitution! We'll get to vote in November just like men."

Women couldn't vote until 1920? That was a new one on me.

Addie rummaged around in a box behind the bar until she found a fancy-looking sports jacket.

"Who does this belong to?" I asked as she helped me put it on.

"Some drunk ran outta here in his underwear," she told me. "He won't be comin' back. You can have it."

She stepped back to look me over. "Pretty spiffy! Fits you like a glove. Now you're hip to the jive, Stoshie! So, where's the stuff?"

"I don't have any stuff," I said.

"C'mon, level with me, Stoshie," she said. "They told me a kid was bringing the stuff."

"I don't know what stuff you're talking about," I told her. She was clearly drunk.

"Then what's a nice young fella like you doing in a juice joint like this?" she asked.

"I'm looking for Carl Mays," I said. "Do you know where he is?"

Addie burst out laughing.

"What's so funny?" I asked.

"C'mere."

She grabbed my hand again and dragged me across the room. People were stumbling all over themselves, laughing crazily and staggering around in a stupor.

"What's going on here?" I asked Addie. "Why is everybody so drunk?"

"Don't ya have Prohibition in Louisville?" Addie asked me. "Hootch is against the law, y'know. We ain't had a legal drink in months. It's only a matter of time before the cops shut this joint down. We're enjoying it while we can."

I learned about Prohibition in Social Studies. For years, alcohol was illegal in the United States. If the police showed up at this place, I'd be in big trouble.

As Addie pulled me across the room, I almost crashed into a guy who was weaving around with a lamp shade on his head.

"Look, I just need to find Carl Mays," I told Addie. "Is he here?"

"Nah, he ain't here," she replied.

"But you know who he is?" I asked.

"Sure I do," Addie said. "He's that pitcher with the Yankees."

"Why did you laugh when I asked if he was here?" I said.

"Carl is such a killjoy," she told me. "I don't think he ever let a sip of booze pass his lips, even when it *was* legal."

Something didn't make sense. This place was a speakeasy, one of those illegal bars. But Carl Mays didn't drink. I wondered why I ended up in a place like this. Finally, Addie pulled me over to a booth where some people were sitting.

"Carl Mays ain't here," she said, "but one of his teammates is. He came over from the Red Sox too. He's only been with the team for a few months, but he's pretty popular. He's sitting right over there."

I recognized that guy.

8

Babe & Me

IT WAS BABE RUTH!

Babe freaking Ruth!

I was paralyzed. I couldn't breathe. Babe Ruth was sitting right in front of me!

Of course! I should have known. The Red Sox sold Babe to the Yankees after the 1919 season. So he started his career with New York in 1920. That meant that he was probably on the field at the moment Ray Chapman was hit.

I shouldn't have been so shocked to see the Babe. We had met before. In fact, I'd met him *twice*. The first time was when I went back to see Jackie Robinson in 1947 and bumped into Babe sitting in the stands at the World Series. Another time I went back to 1932 to see with my own eyes whether or not Babe really called his famous "Called Shot" home run.

But those are stories for another day.

I couldn't help but stare at him. Babe wasn't fat, the way he was in 1932. And he wasn't old and dying, the way he was in 1947. He looked like a big kid, lean and muscular. You could almost call him handsome.

Babe didn't notice me staring at him. He had a lot of distractions. There were two ladies sitting on his knees, a beer in each of his hands, and a plate of spaghetti on the table in front of him. Oh, yeah, and a cigar in his mouth. I don't know how he managed to eat, drink, smoke, and joke with the girls all at the same time; but he seemed to be managing. The girls were laughing, the spaghetti and beer were disappearing like they were being dumped into a bottomless pit, and thick clouds of smoke billowed every time he took a puff on the cigar. My eyes teared, and I reminded myself that it was only recently that smoking was banned in most indoor spaces.

"How's about I hit a homer for each of you pretty girls today?" Babe suggested.

"That would be swell, Babe!" they agreed, and collapsed into giggles.

Babe Ruth was like the sun—everything revolved around him. A waiter came over and refilled his glasses the instant they were empty.

Addie, who had brought me over to the table, had flitted off to talk to somebody else. I guess she figured Babe would take me to Carl Mays.

"Say, here's a riddle for you dolls," Babe said. "Why is it faster to run from first base to second than it is to run from second base to third?"

"Gee whiz, Babe, I dunno!" one of the girls said, giggling.

"Because there's a short stop in the middle," I said.

The girls didn't laugh. Babe didn't say anything. They all just looked at me.

Oops. I wished there was a hole in the floor I could jump into.

But then, Babe busted out laughing.

"That's right!" he said, pounding the table with his fist. "Hey, what's your name, kid?"

"Stosh," I told him, "Joe Stoshack. I'm a big fan, Babe."

"You don't look so big to me!" he said, roaring at his own joke. Then he tilted his head back and half of his beer vanished, like he didn't even need to swallow.

"Gee, Babe, maybe you shouldn't be drinking so much," I suggested gently.

"Who are you, my mother?" Babe said. "Drinking helps me hit homers!"

"Howdya figger that, Babe?" asked one of the girls.

"Well, I hit 29 homers last year for Boston," Babe said. "That's the most ever. And since I moved to New York, I drink a lot more beer. Well, I got 42 homers right now, and the season ain't over yet. So I figger it must be the beer."

The girls cackled, and Babe threw back his head, draining the other glass. I was about to ask him about Carl Mays, but there was a commotion at the other end of the club. Babe stood up to see what it was. The girls hopped off his lap and scurried away, like it was the end of their shift.

"Hey, Harry!" Babe yelled. "Come on over here!"

This had to be my lucky day! Harry Houdini, the guy who I had just seen hanging upside down, was walking toward us.

Houdini was a short man with graying hair and strange-looking eyes. Even though he was fully dressed, you could see he had thick muscles on his arms and legs.

Babe greeted Houdini warmly and introduced me as his new friend.

"I'm pleased to make your acquaintance," Houdini said mysteriously, gripping my hand in a death grip that lasted just a bit too long. He was weirding me out.

"Whatcha drinkin', Harry?" asked Babe.

"I never touch alcohol," Houdini replied.

"Ya don't have to touch it to drink it!" Babe hollered. "Hey, I gotta take a leak. Do that thing you do with the needles, Harry. The kid'll love it."

Babe left, and Houdini pulled a handful of sewing needles out of his pocket. Why anybody would carry around a pocketful of sewing needles is a mystery to me. *Everything* about this guy was a mystery to me.

What happened next was even stranger. Houdini took the needles and popped them into his mouth, like peanuts! Then, he started chewing them! Truly weird. But wait, it gets even weirder.

Houdini picked up a glass of water from the table and guzzled it, as if he was washing down the needles. Then as he looked me in the eye, he pulled a ball of thread out of his pocket. He popped that in his mouth and swallowed it too.

But what happened next was *really* unbelievable. Houdini reached into his mouth and pulled out the thread. That's not the unbelievable part. The unbelievable part was that the thread came out in a line—with all those needles attached to it! He had threaded the needles while they were in his *mouth*!

Houdini could do some weird stuff.

It was *amazing*!

When he was done, Houdini looked at me with an eerie smile and asked if I had seen him "hanging around" outside.

"Yeah," I said. "How did you get out of that strait-jacket?"

"A magician never reveals his secrets," he told me. Then he leaned over and whispered in my ear, "But between you and me, I dislocated my shoulder."

"On *purpose*?" I asked.

"But of course," he replied, and looked at me as if that was a perfectly normal thing to do.

I told Houdini that I had dislocated my shoulder too when I fell down after getting hit by a baseball. He said that after you dislocate your shoulder once, it's easier to do again.

Just talking about stuff like that was creeping me out. Houdini seemed like an alien from outer space who was trying to blend in with the earthlings but wasn't quite pulling it off.

He took a tiny key out of his pocket and slipped it into my hand.

"A souvenir of our meeting," he said. "It will open virtually any lock known to man. You never know when it might come in handy. I hide it in my mouth."

Cool. I thanked him as I slipped the key in my back pocket. Babe came back from the bathroom with a new cigar in his hand. Houdini asked him what time it was.

"Time for another beer!" Babe bellowed.

"Don't you have a game at three thirty?" asked Houdini.

Babe stopped, stared, let out a curse, and quickly grabbed my hand.

"You're right!" he said. "Let's go, kid! We gotta get to the Polo Grounds fast!"

"We?" I asked.

"If anybody asks why I'm late, you're gonna tell 'em I was visiting you in the hospital. Because you're a sick kid and you're dying, okay?"

"But I'm not dying," I protested.

"You're *gonna* be if Hug finds out I was drinking. Let's go!"

Hug? Who's Hug?

There was no time for questions. Babe grabbed a bag from under the table and ran for the door like he was trying to stretch a single into a double. I grabbed my bag with the batting helmet in it and ran after him.

9

A Simple Solution

BABE RUTH DID SOMETHING I HAD NEVER SEEN ANOTHER human being do. He changed clothes while he was running!

It was *amazing*. While we were hustling through the nightclub, Babe somehow tore off his pants and shirt and tossed them aside. Then he reached into the bag he was carrying, took out his Yankees uniform, and put it on—*while* he was hopping around, dodging waiters and various drunks! I don't know how he did it.

And the strange thing was that the people in the club weren't particularly shocked. They acted like that sort of thing went on all the time.

"Hurry up!" he yelled to me as if it was my fault he would be late. "We gotta get to the Polo Grounds!" I could barely keep up with him, and I didn't have to change my clothes.

When we got outside, Babe looked around frantically for a taxi, but there wasn't one on the street. Suddenly, two kids on bikes came pedaling around the corner. Babe jumped in front of them, and they hit their brakes so they wouldn't crash into him.

"It's Babe Ruth!" one of the kids shouted.

"Hey, kids, how much for the bicycles?" asked Babe.

"Huh?" the kids said.

"Here," Babe said, pulling a $20 bill out of his pocket. "We need those bikes."

The kids were still in shock, but they got off their bikes and took the twenty like they had just won the lottery. In 1920, twenty dollars was probably like a thousand.

"Y'know how to ride a bicycle?" Babe asked me.

"Well, sure . . ."

"Then let's go!"

Back when I visited him in 1932, Babe Ruth drove me to Wrigley Field in Chicago. I almost died. Well, he rode a bicycle the same way—like a maniac. He took off and started pedaling furiously, weaving around street vendors, potholes, and garbage cans. Little old ladies were diving out of his way. Cars were honking at him, and I wasn't sure if it was because the drivers recognized Babe Ruth or because some nut on a bike had just cut them off.

I was pedaling as hard as I could to keep up. My heart was racing. I wished I had put on the batting helmet I'd brought for Ray Chapman. If I fell and hit

Babe took off and started pedaling furiously.

my head on the street, there was probably no doctor in 1920 who could help me.

Like I said, I had been to New York a few times now, so it wasn't completely new and different to me. I barely looked at the old-time streetlights, cars, and signs as we zipped by them. Besides, I was too busy trying to avoid hitting them. We sped past a huge movie theater playing *Dr. Jekyll and Mr. Hyde* starring John Barrymore. Whoever he was.

We crossed 125th Street and then 134th Street. I remembered from my last trip that the Polo Grounds was at 157th Street. As we got close, there were fewer stores, cars, or people on the street. I could feel my heartbeat slowing down slightly.

Finally, we came to a sign that said WELCOME TO THE POLO GROUNDS, and I could see the ballpark as we looked down on it from the hill. The Polo Grounds looked pretty much the same as it did when I saw it in 1913. There were players on the field and fans all over. It looked like batting practice was still going on. Lucky for Babe, the game hadn't started yet.

Babe tossed aside the bike the same way he tossed aside his clothes. To Babe Ruth, I guess everything was disposable.

He wasn't out of breath, not like I was. He grabbed my hand and pulled me toward an unmarked door at the side of the ballpark.

"Whatcha got in the bag, kid?" he asked, as we hustled for the door. "Ya got anything to eat in there?"

"It's a batting helmet," I replied, amazed that Babe could still be hungry.

"A helmet that bats?" he asked. "Sounds like a crazy idea to me."

The door was an entrance just for the players; but there was a small group of fans hanging around, waiting for Babe. As soon as they saw him, they surrounded him with pens and papers.

"Sorry, folks. Not now," Babe apologized as we ran through the doorway. "I'm late. See you after the game, okay?"

He led me to the locker room, where there were a bunch of players hanging out, playing checkers and cards. They were already in their uniforms—the old, baggy, flannel kind that players used to wear. Above the lockers I noticed some names I had heard before: Bob Meusel, Ping Bodie, Roger Peckinpaugh.

"Ruth! You're late!"

The high-pitched voice came from a tiny man with big ears. He wasn't much taller than me, and I'm only 5 feet 3 inches. His uniform looked two sizes too big on him. It was almost funny watching the guy yell at Babe Ruth. He was so small, he looked like he could be a ventriloquist's dummy.

"Ah, keep your shirt on, Hug," Babe said. "I'm here, ain't I? The game didn't start yet."

Hug. I remembered that there used to be a manager named Miller Huggins. He is in the Baseball Hall of Fame.

"I need you to be here *two hours* before game time,

Miller Huggins

Ruth!" Huggins said, wagging his finger in Babe's face. "That's the rule."

"Aw, c'mon, Hug, my friend here is dyin'!" Babe said, throwing me a wink. "I had to visit him in the hospital. Ain't that right, kid? What's your name again? Stash?"

"Uh, yes," I said, coughing loudly. "Stosh."

"Yeah, Stosh," Babe said. "The kid has . . ."

"Cancer," I said.

"Right, cancer," said the Babe. "Poor kid has cancer. He's real sick, Hug."

"He don't look sick to *me*," Huggins said, looking me up and down suspiciously.

"Oh, he *looks* fine," Babe explained, "but he's about to drop dead. He probably won't make it through the weekend."

"How come every kid you know is dyin', Ruth?" Huggins demanded. "Every day you come in here late with a new kid who's dyin'. Don'tcha ever meet any kids who ain't dyin'?"

"Sure, Hug. I don't just meet sick kids."

"Maybe the kid's just sick of *you*," Huggins said. "I know I am. Hey, what's in that bag, kid?"

"That's his medicine," Babe said before I could answer. "Keep your paws off."

"Medicine?" Huggins wasn't buying it. "Looks like a lot of medicine for one kid."

"I told you, Hug, the kid is about to drop dead!" Babe said. "He needs a *lotta* medicine. But I'm gonna hit a homer for him today. That oughta make him feel better. Ain't that right, kid?"

"Sure, Babe!"

"Hey, Ruth!" hollered one of the players. "How's the kid gonna feel when you strike out three times like yesterday?"

"Ah, stop flappin' yer gums!" Babe hollered back. "I'm gonna get me a rubdown."

Babe wandered off to the trainer's room and left me standing in the middle of the locker room. I guess I was disposable too. I looked around. One of these guys had to be Carl Mays; but none of them had names or numbers on their uniforms, so I didn't know which one he was.

"Hey, kid," somebody behind me said. I turned around to see a tall player writing on a baseball. "I hope you don't drop dead or nothin'."

He handed me the ball. It had red and blue stitching on it. I turned it around. On the other side was this . . .

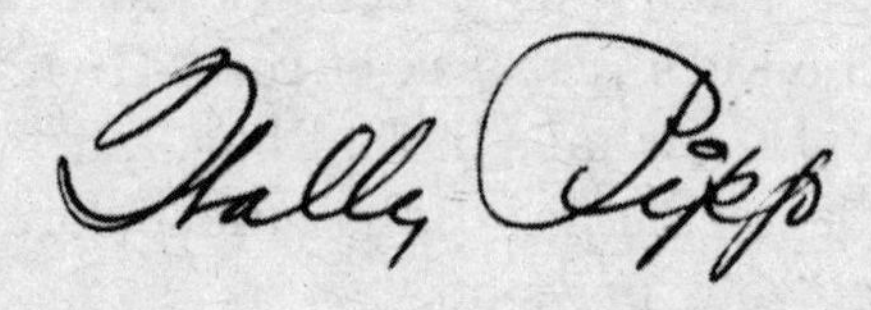

WALLY PIPP!? I remembered that name. He was the guy Flip told us about! Flip said Pipp played for the Yankees in the 1920s. And here he was!

"You play first base, right?" I asked.

"That's right," Pipp said.

Wally Pipp

"Listen, uh, this is gonna sound a little nutty," I told him, "but don't ever ask for a day off, okay?"

"Huh?" Pipp said. "Why not?"

"You're not gonna believe this," I explained, "but in a few years, you're gonna have a headache. And you're gonna ask for a day off. And some young guy named Lou Gehrig is gonna take your place that day. And he's gonna be so good that he's gonna take your job. And the Yankees are gonna sell you to Cincinnati. Trust me on this."

Wally Pipp looked at me like I was crazy.

"How would *you* know what's gonna happen in a few years?" he asked. "I never even *heard* of nobody named Gehrig. You really *are* sick, kid. Maybe you better get back to the hospital."

I could have tried to convince Wally Pipp not to ask for a day off. I could have argued with him. But there was no point. My mom always told me that you've got to choose your battles in life. I had more important things to do than save Wally Pipp's career.

"Forget it," I told Pipp. "Thanks for the ball. Can you tell me where I might find Carl Mays?"

Pipp pointed to a locker all the way in the corner of the clubhouse.

"Over there," Pipp told me. "But don't bother him. He don't like bein' bothered. Especially today. He's going for his 100th career victory."

Carl Mays was sitting on a bench by himself, hunched over with his back to me. He was stripped to the waist, wearing gym shorts. He looked lost in thought. His foot was nervously tapping the floor.

As I got closer, I could see there was a scar on the back of his left leg, maybe six inches long. On the floor of his locker were four pairs of baseball shoes, all shined up and lined up perfectly in a row. There were a few bats leaning against the wall behind me, also perfectly in a line. He must have been a neat freak.

Suddenly, I had an incredible idea. I could accomplish my mission right here and now. I didn't have to give a batting helmet to Ray Chapman to save his life. All I had to do was pick up one of those bats and whack Carl Mays on his pitching arm with it!

If he was injured, he wouldn't be able to play. And if he wasn't able to play, he wouldn't be able to hit Ray Chapman in the head with a ball. And if he didn't hit Chapman with the ball . . . well, you get the idea.

It would be so *easy*!

My mind was racing, but I had to think this thing through. If I whacked Mays with the bat, the rest of the Yankees would surely surround me in about two seconds and beat the crap out of me. I'd most likely get arrested and possibly thrown in jail. If they took away my new pack of baseball cards, there would be no way for me to get back home again. I'd be stuck in 1920 forever.

It was a dilemma. If I whacked Mays with the bat, I would be saving Ray Chapman's life and possibly ruining my own. Is it the right thing to do to hurt somebody if it would save somebody else's life? I didn't know.

I eyed the bats. I could always argue that by hitting Mays with a bat, I was saving *two* lives. Chapman wouldn't die, and Mays wouldn't have to go through the rest of his life knowing that he killed Chapman.

But who would believe me afterward when I explained that I was only trying to help these guys? I was the only person in 1920 who knew that Ray Chapman was going to be dead in a matter of hours. Nobody else had a clue. They would just think I was some crazy kid who attacked Carl Mays with a bat.

There wasn't a lot of time to work out all the consequences. I had to make a decision fast.

I put down the ball that Wally Pipp gave me. I picked up one of Carl Mays's bats.

10

All Part of the Game

In the end, I didn't have to decide whether or not to attack Carl Mays with his own baseball bat. Because at that moment, he turned around and looked at me.

I could have swung the bat, anyway. Mays would have been so surprised, he probably wouldn't have been able to block it. I could have smashed his pitching arm, made a run for the door, and maybe even gotten out of there before the whole Yankee team grabbed me.

But I couldn't bring myself to do it. Maybe hitting him *was* the right thing to do, but it's just not in my nature to hit an innocent man with a baseball bat.

"What are you doin' with my bat?" Mays asked.

I was sure he was going to kill me. He had every right to kill me. Ballplayers are very protective about their bats and gloves. Hey, I don't like strangers touching my stuff either. He probably *would* have killed me too if he knew what I had been thinking about.

"I'm . . . uh . . . just admiring it," I stammered. "What is this, 32 ounces?"

"33," he replied, taking the bat from me.

Mays was a big guy, with broad, muscular shoulders. He had short blond hair, not quite a crew cut. Blue eyes. Sharp nose. He wore a grimace on his face that looked permanent. It was like he had a toothache or something.

I desperately tried to think of something to say to the man so he wouldn't think I had been on the verge of whacking him with his own bat.

"What happened to your leg?" I asked.

Mays looked down at his scar and touched it.

"That's a little artwork courtesy of a fellow named Ty Cobb," he said. "He bunted a ball down the first-base line on me. I scooped it up. When I went to tag him, he spiked me pretty good."

"What a jerk," I said. It wasn't the first time I had heard about Cobb hurting someone on purpose.

"It's all part of the game, son," Mays told me, "all part of the game."

I wanted to talk to Mays about Ray Chapman, but I didn't quite know how to get started. How do you tell a man that in a few hours, he's going to do something that will result in another man's death and change his own life forever? He'd never believe me.

Carl Mays

Carl Mays didn't tell me to get lost, but he didn't ask me to stay either. He reached into his locker, took out something, and put it in his mouth.

"What's that?" I asked.

"A chicken neck," he said. "Keeps my mouth moist."

Okay! So the guy was a little eccentric. That didn't make him a bad guy. It certainly didn't make him a murderer. He turned back around to face his locker.

"Uh, Mr. Mays?" I asked. I had to say *something*.

"Yeah?" he said, turning around again and taking the chicken neck out of his mouth.

"Be careful out there today," I said.

"I'm always careful," he replied, and then he went back to sucking on his chicken neck.

I wasn't going to get anywhere with Carl Mays. I decided to stick with my original plan—to find Ray Chapman and give him my batting helmet. Then I'd go home and see if I had changed history.

As I headed for the door, Babe Ruth strolled out of the trainer's room, wearing only a towel and puffing on a cigar.

"Swing big and hit big," Babe was telling one of the other players. "That's why I led the league in homers the last two years. You know how many I hit for the Sox last season? 29. And you know how many the whole *team* hit? 33! That's a fact. Just four more. And that's why I'm making ten grand this year. Swing big, hit big, and earn big."

Suddenly, I noticed Carl Mays got up off the bench in front of his locker.

"Why don't you shut your cake hole for once in your life, Ruth?" Mays said.

All the locker-room conversation and card games stopped instantly. Silence. It was like a cemetery in there. Everybody was staring at Carl Mays. And then, like they were watching a game of tennis, all heads swiveled over to Ruth.

"Who's gonna make me?" the Babe said, striding over to Mays.

The two men were right in each other's faces. Mays looked a couple of inches shorter than the Babe, but just as strong.

"Easy, boys," one of the players said.

"You were born with a *gift*, Ruth," Mays said. "The rest of us would give *anything* to have your talent. But you're just wasting it. How many home runs would you hit if you didn't spend all your time drinking and smoking and chasing girls? Why don't you try getting a good night's sleep for once? Why don't you try to help this team win the pennant?"

"Why don't you mind your own business, Carl?" Babe shot back.

"This *is* my business, Ruth," Mays said. "I want to win the pennant. I want to win the World Series. Just like every man in this room does. And we're not gonna win *anything* if you don't shape up."

"You're just jealous, Carl!" Ruth shouted. "You were jealous of me when we were on the Red Sox, and you're jealous of me now."

"You're drunk!" Mays said.

"And you're chicken!" Ruth barked. "Is that why you suck on a chicken neck? Maybe *you* should take a drink once in a while. It might loosen you up."

"I'm plenty loose," Mays said. And with that, he hauled off and socked Babe Ruth in the jaw.

Babe got a punch or two in before the rest of the Yankees jumped on the players and pulled them apart. I hoped that Babe might hit Mays in his pitching arm and put him out of the game, but he didn't.

While the Yankees were still yelling and shouting at each other, I decided it might be a good time to remove myself from the situation. I made my way to the locker-room door and slipped out of there.

11

Nice Hat

WHEN I WALKED OUT OF THE YANKEES LOCKER ROOM, I realized that I'd left my baseball behind. Too late now. Fists were flying in there. I wasn't going back. Not for a Wally Pipp ball. If Babe had signed it—well, that would be another story.

I found myself in a dimly lit corridor somewhere in the bowels of the Polo Grounds. A few doors down was a sign with the word VISITORS on it. I thought the door would be locked, but it wasn't. I looked left and right. Nobody was around, so I pulled open the door and went inside.

The locker room was empty. The Indians were probably still taking infield practice. They might freak out if they came into their locker room and found a strange kid there. I needed a place to hide.

I opened one of the wooden lockers. It was stuffed with gloves and bats and balls and other gear. I opened a few more lockers until I found one that was empty. Perfect. I got in and closed the door behind me.

I waited. There were some thin slots I could look through. I wondered—would I recognize Ray Chapman from the pictures I'd seen of him? I rehearsed in my mind what I was going to say to him.

This was not the first time I found myself hiding in a locker room, it occurred to me. One time, I was on a mission to visit Mickey Mantle in 1951, but I got blown off course and ended up in 1944—in the locker room of an all-girls' baseball team. But that's a story for another day.

Footsteps. Voices. A bunch of players piled into the room. I peered through the slot in the door. The word CLEVELAND went across their uniforms. I prayed that nobody would open the locker I was hiding in. That would be embarrassing. I kept looking for Ray Chapman.

The atmosphere in the Indian locker room was completely different. These guys were laughing, happy, clapping each other on the back. One of them suddenly started to sing, and the others gathered around him to join in.

Sweet Adeline,
My Adeline,
At night, dear heart,
For you I pine.
In all my dreams,
Your fair face beams.

You're the flower of my heart,
Sweet Adeline.

"Sweet Adeline"! I remembered that girl I'd met in the speakeasy. She said her name was Adeline, just like the song.

It was a style of music you hardly ever hear anymore. Really slow, with a lot of harmony. I think they call it "barbershop music," because it would usually be sung by men who were hanging out in a barbershop. It actually sounded good. Some of the Indians put their hands over their hearts as they sang.

The Indians started singing "Sweet Adeline."

When the song was over, the players laughed and gathered around one guy with silver hair. He looked a little older than the others, but not old. I guess he was the manager of the team.

"Speaker will speak!" somebody announced.

Speaker. I recalled that name because it was unusual. Tris Speaker. He's in the Baseball Hall of Fame. He was a great centerfielder and led the American League in batting one year. In his playing days, he was a rival of Ty Cobb. Maybe, I guessed, he was a player-manager.

"Fellas, we need this one today," he said in a thick Texas accent. "We've been doin' great. We're 70 and 40 right now. But the Sox are right behind us. And remember when these Yanks beat us four in a row last week in Cleveland? Can't let that happen again."

"Ruth is tough," one of the Indians said. "You make one mistake to him, and he hits it over the wall."

"Ruth is just a man," Speaker said. "He puts his pants on one leg at a time, just like you 'n' me. And last year he struck out twice as many times as he homered. You can look it up."

Speaker threw his arms around the players on either side of him.

"Boys," he said quietly, "y'know, since our club was formed back in 1879, we ain't won a single pennant. That's 40 years. Not one pennant. Neither did those Yanks, so they want it just as bad as us. We finished

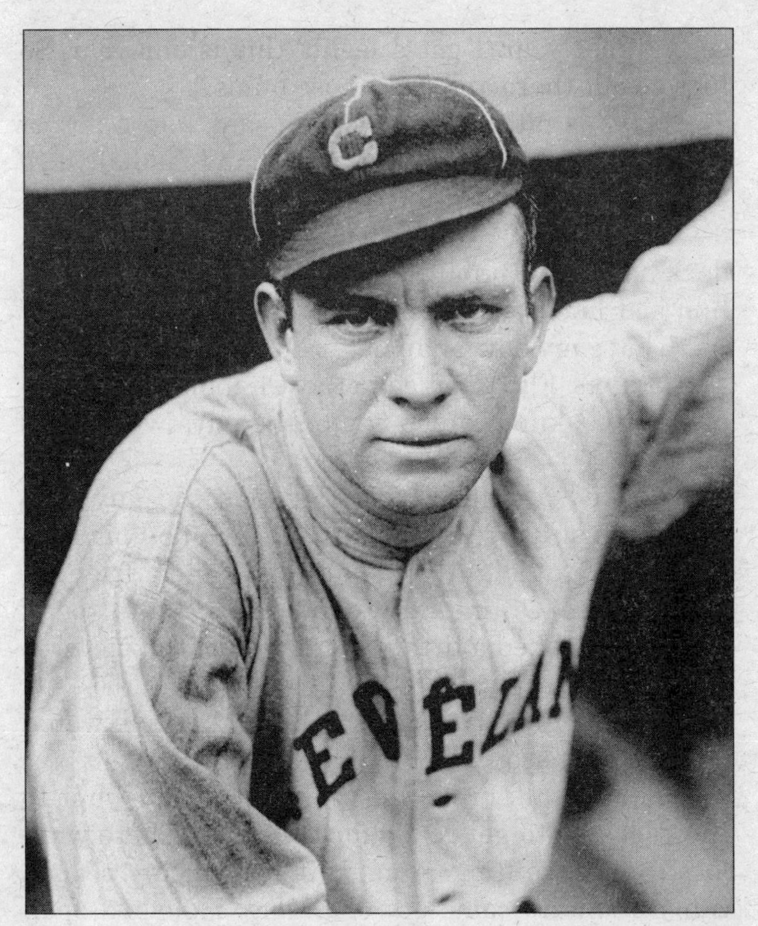

Tris Speaker

second last year. I got a feelin' this is our year. So let's go out there and *beat* those bums."

"Mays is pitching," somebody said, and a few of the Indians groaned. "That underhand fastball sure is hard to pick up."

"Mays doesn't bother me," said a slim guy with dark hair, as he unbuttoned his uniform top. "We hit him just like we hit everybody else."

"That's my boy, Chappie!" said Speaker.

Chappie. Flip referred to Ray Chapman as "Chappie." Now I knew which one of the guys was Chapman.

I looked at him closely. He was the guy who started in singing "Sweet Adeline." He had big ears that stuck out slightly, a square jaw, and a friendly, smiling face. On his right shoulder was a tattoo of a bird. He looked a little different from the pictures I had seen.

If I didn't do anything, I realized, this man would be dead very soon.

The pep talk broke up, and the players went to their lockers to get ready for the game. There were lots of guys milling around. It looked like a good time for me to come out of hiding. I pushed open the locker door and pretended to be a clubhouse attendant. Baseball teams *always* need a clubhouse attendant, because baseball players are slobs who leave a big mess that *somebody's* got to clean up. There was a broom in the corner. I grabbed it and started sweeping.

I swept around the locker room until I found Ray Chapman's locker over in the corner. He was sitting on a bench going through a stack of fan mail. He didn't pay any attention to me.

The door to Chapman's locker was open, and there was a photo taped to it. I got as close as I could without being too obvious and then strained my eyes to see the photo. It was a picture of a bride and groom. The girl was pretty. Even though the photo was black-and-white, I could tell she had light brown hair. Below the photo were these words:

Kathleen and Ray, October 29, 1919

I did a rough calculation in my head. Ray Chapman and his wife got married eight months earlier.

I had waited a long time for this moment. At any second, the players could be called out to the field to start the game. This might be my only chance to talk with Ray Chapman one-on-one. I worked up my courage.

"Excuse me, Mr. Chapman?" I asked quietly.

"Yes, son?" he said, looking up at me with kindly eyes. He had no accent. I remembered that Flip said he came from Kentucky, like me.

"I want to give you something," I said. I pulled the batting helmet out of my bag and handed it to him.

"What the heck is *this* contraption?"

"It's a helmet," I began. "This is going to be hard for me to explain; but in the game today, Mr. Chapman, you could get hit. I mean, you're *going* to get hit. Hard. In the head."

Ray looked at the helmet, turning it over in his hands. He tapped it with his knuckles.

"Where'd you get this thing?" he asked.

"I . . . uh, had it in my garage," I explained.

"How do you know so much about the game today?" he asked, smile lines forming at the corners of his eyes. "Where's your crystal ball? Are you one of those fellas who predicts the future?"

"Not exactly . . ."

What could I say? That I came from the future? He'd never believe the truth in a million years. A lie was more believable.

". . . I get hunches about things," I continued. "I've got a hunch that if you wear this helmet when you're batting today, it will save your life."

"Are you crazy, son?" he asked. "Because you sure sound crazy."

"I'm not crazy," I explained. "I'm—"

Ray Chapman took my batting helmet and put it on his head. It fit. He stood up and laughed.

"Hey, fellas!" he shouted. "Look at this!"

Tris Speaker and some of the other Indians came over.

"Nice hat, Chappie!" somebody said, and they all broke up laughing.

"This young fella says it'll protect me when I'm hitting," said Chapman.

"You might as well wear a dress too, Chappie!" somebody said, which caused the Indians to double over.

Ray took off the helmet and tapped it with his fingernails.

"What's this thing made of?" he asked.

"Plastic," I answered, instantly regretting it.

"Plastic?" Ray snorted. "What's plastic?"

"It's this really strong stuff," I said. "But it's not too heavy."

"Strong?" Speaker said, grabbing a bat from Ray's locker. "Let's see. Toss that thing to me, Chappie."

Speaker got into a batting stance, and everybody stood back to give him room. Ray underhanded my batting helmet to him from about ten feet away. Speaker took a full swing.

Crrrrraaaaaaaaaaaaaaccccccccckkkkkkk.

Pieces of my batting helmet went flying across the locker room. The Indians collapsed all over each other in hysterics.

"It don't look so strong to me," Speaker said.

So much for *that* idea. I had blown my mission. Again.

12

The Good Old Days

STUPID! THAT'S WHAT I WAS. STUPID!

What was I thinking? That a player in 1920 would just willingly put on a batting helmet with no questions asked?

I should have known better. I mean, I don't know as much about baseball history as Flip, but I do know that athletes didn't start wearing protective gear for a long, long time. My dad once told me that when he was a kid, hockey players didn't wear helmets. It wasn't considered "manly." Baseball players didn't even wear *gloves* when the game began.

Bringing Ray Chapman a batting helmet was a dumb idea. I might as well have brought him a cell phone.

The Indians must have thought that busting up my helmet was the funniest thing they'd ever seen. While they fell all over themselves laughing, I slinked out of the locker room. Nobody seemed to care.

Why do I do this? I asked myself as I wandered through the tunnels of the Polo Grounds, looking for an exit. *Why do I take it upon myself to save the world?* Nobody cares. Even if I was able to change history, nobody would notice. Because they would never know what would have happened if I had left things the way they were.

I should have whacked Carl Mays with a bat when I had the chance. That would have been the simple solution. Heck, I could have whacked *Ray Chapman* with a bat and knocked him out of the lineup! That would have saved his life too.

I was disgusted. I figured I'd just find a quiet spot, take out one of my new baseball cards, and go home. There was no point in hanging around the Polo Grounds any longer. Chalk it up to experience.

But suddenly, I caught a whiff of something. Something good. It was the smell of roasted peanuts. Man, that's a good smell! They don't roast them at the ballpark anymore. Now you just buy peanuts in plastic bags. It's not the same.

I didn't have any money, but I couldn't resist following the smell. It led me to a door; and when I pulled it open, there was the field.

You can talk all you want about the Grand Canyon, the pyramids, and all those other wonders of the world. But for me, there's nothing more beautiful than walking up the ramp to see the grass of a ball field. It just hits you in the face with green.

I'll just stay for a couple of innings, I told myself.

It was my dad who'd taught me the fine art of "sneaking down" at a ball game. He could never afford good seats, so he would buy the cheapest tickets available. Then, inning by inning, we would sneak our way closer to the field as we spotted better seats that nobody was sitting in. By the ninth inning, we would usually be in the first row. Of course, that was before he got hurt.

It's even easier to sneak down when you're alone, because you don't have to find two seats together.

I grabbed the first empty seat I saw, to establish a base of operations, and scoped out the Polo Grounds from there.

The ballpark was about three quarters full. It looked pretty much like a modern-day ballpark, with a few exceptions. Foul territory was really big. There was a narrow dirt path leading from home plate to the pitcher's mound. Old-time cars were parked beyond the outfield. Ads on the fences were for products that didn't exist anymore, like THE EVER READY SAFETY RAZOR. And all the men in the stands were wearing straw hats. Nobody wears hats anymore in the summertime. I wondered why they ever wore them in the first place.

I had to be careful sneaking down. There were security guards roaming around. And they weren't old, retired guys like the security guards at home. These were big, ugly guys with police nightsticks. Getting caught by one of them would not be a good thing.

Carefully, I moved down a few rows, ping-ponging my way from one seat to the next one. Finally, I found a nice location—about ten rows off the field and directly behind the Yankees dugout. I plopped down in a seat next to a kid with red hair. He looked about my age.

"Hey, that's my sister's seat," he said to me.

"Is she coming back?" I asked.

"She didn't come at all," he replied. "My sister hates baseball."

I turned to look at the kid. He had so many freckles on his face that it looked like one big freckle. The kid had more freckle than he had face. He said his name was Ronnie.

Ronnie was clearly a serious fan. He had a scorecard on his lap and a bunch of baseball cards in one hand.

"This is a good spot to catch a foul ball," I pointed out to Ronnie. He just looked at me. The kid was weird.

Vendors came around hawking hot dogs and soda pop for five cents. Five cents! Too bad I didn't have a penny. Ronnie got up and cheered as the Yankees took the field. A light rain began to fall. Not enough to hold up the game though.

The first thing I noticed was the players' gloves. They were tiny, and there were no laces holding the fingers together. It looked like it would be very hard to catch a ball with one of those things.

Ronnie stood up and cheered when Carl Mays walked slowly to the mound and started to warm up.

Carl Mays was a submariner, and he nearly scraped his knuckles against the ground before releasing the ball.

I had seen video of other pitchers who threw underhand—Ted Abernathy, Dan Quisenberry. The motion is strange. As he wound up, Mays sort of hid the ball behind him until the last possible moment. Then he swung his arm down and just about scraped his knuckles against the ground as he slingshotted the ball to the plate. I sure wouldn't want to look at a fastball coming at me from that angle. Mays threw hard, and grunted so loud with each pitch that you could hear it in the stands. Just watching him pitch made me sweat.

"Mays is going for his 100th win today," I said, trying to show Ronnie that I knew a thing or two.

"Everybody knows that," he replied.

The crowd stood up while a band played the national anthem. A guy with a megaphone came out and announced that Charlie Jamieson would lead off for the Indians.

"Boo!" Ronnie yelled. "Indians stink!"

Jamieson came out of the Cleveland dugout and strode up to the plate. He didn't look like he was intimidated by Carl Mays.

Jamieson swung at the first pitch and fouled it off. Before I knew what was happening, the ball was flying right at me.

"Watch out!" Ronnie yelled.

For maybe a millisecond, I was frozen. All I could do was think about Hammerin' Cameron nailing me in the head with a ball.

At the last possible instant, I unfroze and dove

out of the way. The ball slammed into the back of my wooden seat and bounced off. It was rolling around near my feet. I grabbed it and held it in the air for everybody to see.

I was expecting at least a smattering of polite applause. Nothing. Instead, one of those big security guards hustled over.

"Gimme the ball," he demanded.

"But . . . it's mine," I protested.

"You want I should bust your head open?" he asked, holding up his nightstick. "That ball is the property of the New York Yankees."

I handed him the ball and sat down, humiliated. He threw the ball back on to the field. It rolled near Carl Mays, and he picked it up.

"You thought you could *keep* it?" Ronnie asked, shaking his head. "Ain't ya never been to a ball game?"

Slumping down in my seat, I barely noticed when Jamieson singled. I wondered what year they started letting fans keep foul balls.

"Now batting for Cleveland," the megaphone man boomed, "the shortstop, Ray Chapman!"

Chapman stepped up to the plate. In the fifth inning, in about an hour, he would be a dead man. I was the only one in the world who knew it. And there was nothing I could do about it.

"How's Chapman doing?" I asked Ronnie.

"He's batting .303," he replied, looking at his scorecard, "with three homers and 97 runs scored."

Chapman took a few warm-up swings.

Chapman glanced at the runner on first as he tapped his bat against his spikes. The third baseman moved in three steps, like he was expecting a bunt. Chapman took a couple of warm-up swings, and then he positioned his left foot inches from home plate. His right foot was a few inches back. He held the bat way back and completely motionless. There was no waggle.

Mays wound up, and Chapman squared around to bunt. With Chapman leaning over the plate like that, it looked like it would actually be possible for Mays to throw a strike and still hit him in the head.

The pitch was outside, but Chapman stabbed at it with the bat and dropped a perfect bunt in front of the plate. The catcher pounced on it and threw to first for the out. Jamieson advanced to second.

"Chapman will kill you with those bunts," Ronnie said, as he marked the play on his scorecard. "He's leading the league in sacrifices, again."

The Indians had a runner in scoring position, but they couldn't bring him around. Tris Speaker flied out to centerfield. So did the next Indian. Three outs.

"Mays is looking sharp," Ronnie remarked, as the Yankees jogged off the field. "This could be his lucky day."

"I don't think so," I replied.

The Indians took the field, and the megaphone man announced that their pitcher was Stan Coveleskie. I knew that name, because he is in the Baseball Hall of Fame.

"Boo!" Ronnie yelled. "You stink, Coveleskie!"

Stan Coveleskie was a legal spitballer. When the pitch was banned—just this year, in 1920—he and 16 other guys who were throwing it were allowed to keep throwing it until the end of their careers. After that, there would be no more spitballs. Or legal ones, anyway.

Before each pitch, Coveleskie put two fingers in his mouth. That didn't mean he threw the spitter on every pitch, but you never knew *when* he would throw it. That's why he was so hard to hit. Sometimes he pretended to throw the spitter but threw a fastball instead. Pitchers have to be psychologists too.

Anyway, the Yankees couldn't hit Coveleskie. They went down one, two, three in the bottom of the first. The fans got all excited when Babe Ruth came up to bat, but he hit a weak infield pop-up to end the inning.

"You're a big bunch of cheese!" somebody hollered as Ruth ran off the field.

"So's your old man!" he yelled back.

I found myself enjoying the game. Here I was, sitting in the legendary Polo Grounds watching a day game played in 1920. No artificial turf. No designated hitters or steroid-inflated hitters. No exploding scoreboard or fancy computer graphics. This was *real* baseball, the way Flip always told me the game should be played. I was in the middle of the good old days. I wished they would never end.

Stan Coveleskie

One of the interesting things about baseball, they say, is that it has no clock. With football, basketball, soccer, hockey, and most other sports, the game ends when time runs out. But time *never* runs out in baseball. There's no time limit. A team can't build a lead and then just run out the clock. If you could keep getting hits and scoring runs, the game would go on forever.

The Yankees quickly jogged onto the field to start the second inning. They didn't have to wait for the TV commercials to finish. There *was* no TV in 1920. They didn't even have radio yet. This game was going to go fast.

I put my feet up on the seat in front of me and put my hands behind my head. And then reality hit me. I reminded myself—a man is going to die here, very soon.

My dumb plan to supply Ray Chapman with a batting helmet hadn't worked. But I was sitting no more than 30 yards from where Chapman was going to get hit. I couldn't just go home after a few innings. I had to do something. I had to come up with a plan.

If I was going to do anything, I'd have to do it soon. Maybe baseball didn't have a clock, but Ray Chapman's life did. And it was ticking away.

13

A Serious Disturbance

"MAN, BALLPLAYERS SURE SPIT A LOT," RONNIE SAID, AS THE Indians came up to bat in the second inning.

I ignored him. There were other things on my mind. Like saving Ray Chapman's life. I had gone over all the possibilities in my head. There weren't a whole lot of options.

My batting helmet was shattered, so there was no way to protect Chapman's skull from the ball. I would have to come up with a way to stop Mays from throwing the ball in the first place.

I had to distract him. Interrupt the game somehow. Maybe I could throw something on the field. No, that would only postpone the inevitable. I would have to cause some kind of a serious disturbance.

In the twenty-first century, crazy people charge onto ball fields to disrupt games all the time. Usually the cops get to them pretty quickly and drag them away. But charging the field would probably be a novelty in 1920. I bet nobody had ever done that before. The cops wouldn't be able to react in time. That might be my only option at this point.

Then another thought crossed my mind. Streaking! I could streak! That would totally blow their minds if I ripped off my clothes and ran across the field.

No, streaking might be going a bit too far. I would probably be beaten up by people in the stands before I even got my clothes off. And where would I put my new pack of baseball cards? I couldn't lose it.

I looked around. About ten yards away was that security goon who took away my foul ball. He was eyeing me suspiciously.

There was only one thing I had going for me—knowledge. I knew exactly when Chapman would get hit. He would lead off the fifth inning. The third pitch from Mays would hit him in the head.

I was lost in thought when suddenly the Cleveland batter hit a long drive to leftfield. It cleared the fence for a home run.

"Boooooooooooo!" yelled the Yankees crowd.

"Who was that?" I asked Ronnie.

"Steve O'Neill," he replied. "The catcher."

Never heard of him. O'Neill circled the bases to a chorus of boos and was congratulated when he went into the Indian dugout. The fan who caught the ball threw it back onto the field. Ronnie marked the home run in his scorecard. The Indians were ahead, 1-0.

From where I was sitting, I could see that the

baseball they had been using for the first two innings wasn't white anymore. There was dirt and spit all over it. I bet it was hard for a batter to see. But still, the umpire kept it in the game.

"Why do you think ballplayers spit so much?" Ronnie asked me.

"Beats me," I said. "I don't spit when I play."

"Me neither."

He was right, come to think of it. You don't see football players spitting through their face guards very much. Basketball players wouldn't *think* of spitting on the wood floor during a game. But when you watch a baseball game, it seems like the guys are spitting constantly.

"They should keep statistics on spitting," I suggested. "At the end of the year, they could give an award to the guy who spit the most times. That would be cool."

"Cool?" Ronnie said. "Whaddaya mean?"

"Uh . . . swell," I said.

I was looking at Babe Ruth in rightfield. He spit, and I told Ronnie to put a mark on his scorecard next to Ruth's name.

"That's one for Ruth," Ronnie said.

As the next batter stepped up to the plate, Carl Mays spit on the mound. Ronnie recorded it on his scorecard.

"Wally Pipp just spit at first base," I pointed out.

"Peckinpaugh too," Ronnie said, quickly marking it down.

"Does the umpire count?" I asked. "He just spit."

"Why not?"

At the end of the second inning, Cleveland was ahead in the game, 1-0, but the Yankees had the spitting lead, 19-12.

Nobody scored in the third inning. Ray Chapman came up again with a runner at first, but he bunted into a double play. In the fourth, the Indians scored two more runs with a walk, an error, and a single by O'Neill. That made it 3-0. Ray Chapman was on deck when Cleveland made the third out. The Yankees went down weakly in the bottom half of the inning. The home fans were getting restless for their team to do something.

The drizzling rain had stopped. I was having fun keeping the spitting statistics with Ronnie, but now it was crunch time. Ray Chapman would be leading off the fifth inning. I could feel my heart beating faster. I had never run onto a field before to disrupt a game. Causing a disturbance and breaking the law was not my thing.

"Are you okay?" Ronnie said to me. "You're sweatin' like a pig."

"Something bad is happening," I said.

"Yeah, the Yanks are gettin' beat," said Ronnie.

"No, something worse than that."

"There's nothin' worse than that," Ronnie replied.

I glanced at the security guard. If he grabbed me before I reached the field, it would all be over. I needed Ronnie to help me. The Yankees were already coming out of their dugout to take the field.

The security guard was giving me the evil eye. I would have to level with Ronnie. I lowered my voice so the people sitting around us wouldn't hear.

"Listen," I told Ronnie, "I need your help. You're not gonna believe this, but I'm from the twenty-first century."

"What?!"

"This is important," I told him. "I can name every president after World War . . . I mean, after the 1940s. There's gonna be TV and DVD and rock and roll and the Internet and all kinds of other cool . . . I mean swell . . . stuff."

"Are you nuts?" Ronnie asked.

"You gotta believe me," I told him. "Babe Ruth is gonna end his career with 714 home runs, but Hank Aaron and Barry Bonds are gonna hit even more. A guy named Jackie Robinson's gonna break the color barrier. The Dodgers and the Giants are gonna move to California. We're gonna land a man on the moon in 1969. That same year, the Mets are gonna win the World Series."

"The Mets?" Ronnie asked. "Who are the Mets?"

Carl Mays jogged out to the mound to warm up.

"That's not the point!" I told Ronnie. "Chapman is about to lead off. On the third pitch, Mays is gonna hit him in the head."

"So what?" Ronnie said. "Mays hits guys in the head all the time."

"This time he's gonna kill one," I said.

"Who cares?" said Ronnie. "The only good Indian is a dead Indian."

I sat back for a moment. It was mind-boggling to think that somebody could be so selfish.

"Lemme put it in a way you might understand," I said, grabbing Ronnie's shoulder. "Killing Chapman is gonna keep Carl Mays out of the Hall of Fame."

"The Hall of *what*?" Ronnie said. "You're a lunatic."

I was getting nowhere with this kid. I had forgotten that the Baseball Hall of Fame didn't even exist in 1920.

Ray Chapman was coming out of the Cleveland dugout. He had two bats in his hands, and he was swinging them loosely around his body. Mays was tossing in warm-up pitches.

"Listen to me," I said urgently. "I came from the future to save Ray Chapman's life. I need you to cause a distraction. I need you to get that security guy to stop staring at me. Pretend to choke or something. I'm gonna run on the field and tackle Mays just before he throws the third pitch."

Ronnie just looked at me.

"I'm not fooling around!" I said. "In a minute or two, a man is gonna have his head split open right over *there*! Are you gonna help me save him or not?"

"Prove you're from the future," Ronnie said.

Oh, man! I didn't have time for this crap! How could I prove it to him?

I thought of a way. Frantically, I pulled my new

baseball cards out of my pocket.

"Look at this," I said, ripping open the pack. "See this guy? Alex Rodriguez. They call him A-Rod. See the stats on the back? See the year? Here, keep it. I've got plenty more."

Ronnie looked at the card carefully, turning it over and over.

"Okay, okay," he finally said. "What do you want me to do?"

I breathed a sigh of relief.

"When I say so, you distract the security guard," I told Ronnie. "I'm gonna charge the field."

"Now batting for Cleveland," hollered the megaphone man, "the shortstop, Ray Chapman!"

Chapman flung one of the bats toward the Cleveland dugout. He was coming up to the plate. The Yankees were still tossing a ball around the infield. Tris Speaker came out of the dugout and kneeled on deck.

The Yankees catcher squatted down. Chapman set himself in the batter's box and pulled down the brim of his cap slightly. The umpire signaled for Mays to pitch and leaned in behind the catcher. Mays looked in for the sign. Then he nodded, went into his windup, and let it fly.

"Steeeee-rike!" cried the ump.

Chapman didn't step out of the batter's box. He just took a few practice swings. Mays was a fast worker too. He got set to deliver the next pitch and pumped it in.

"Ball one!" cried the ump. A little outside.

One and one count. This was it. The third pitch.

"Okay, you ready?" I said to Ronnie.

"Yeah."

"Go!" I said, bolting out of my seat.

I ran down the aisle toward the field and was about ten feet from the fence when I heard Ronnie shout.

"Officer!" he yelled. "That kid is crazy! Stop him!"

Dammit!

I had my hand on the fence when I was tackled from behind. Then I saw it all like it was in slow motion. . . .

Mays went into his big windup. Chapman shifted his back foot, as if he was going to attempt a push bunt down the first-base line.

The ball was rocketing toward the plate. It had to be a fastball.

The Yankee catcher raised his glove to snare the high pitch.

Chapman wasn't moving. He stood like a statue.

"Duck, Ray!" I shouted.

But he never heard me.

And then I heard the sickening sound of a baseball striking bone.

14

Troublemaker

THE SECURITY GUARD WAS ON TOP OF ME, PUSHING MY face against the concrete floor.

"Owww!" I groaned under his weight. "Easy! I have a bad shoulder!"

"Boo-hoo," he muttered with tobacco breath. "I'm cryin'."

"Can't you see what just happened?" I shouted. "Chapman just got hit!"

The security guard looked up at the field and said, "No he didn't."

I strained to look up through the fence. The ball was rolling slowly between the pitcher's mound and third base. Carl Mays picked it up and threw it to first.

"Yer out!" called the ump.

It looked like nothing unusual had happened. Wally Pipp, the Yankees first baseman, was about to step off the bag and fire the ball around the infield. But then he stopped, frozen.

There was no base runner.

I looked back at home plate. Chapman was still standing there holding the bat in his hands. Then he sank to his knees. His eyes were closed, his mouth slightly open. The bat dropped to the ground.

"Faker!" shouted somebody in the stands. "Those bums'll do anything to get on base!"

"The ball hit his bat!" Mays yelled, as he walked toward the umpire.

Chapman struggled to his feet. He took a few clumsy steps toward the pitcher's mound, as if he was going to charge Mays.

And then he collapsed.

The crowd gasped. The Yankees catcher rushed over to Chapman. So did Tris Speaker, who was on deck. He was the first Indian to get there.

"We need a doctor!" shouted Speaker, waving his arms. "Is there a doctor in the house?"

Suddenly, people were shouting instructions from all directions.

"Somebody get a stretcher!"

"Give him air!"

"Get some water!"

"Get him to a hospital!" I shouted.

I figured the security guard lying on top of me would see that there were more important things to deal with than a crazy kid charging the field. But he wouldn't release his grip on me.

"All right, show's over, pal," he said, grabbing the back of my neck. "You're coming with me."

"What did I do?" I protested. "I didn't do anything!"

As he dragged me up the steps, I could see the Indians rushing out of their dugout, and some of the Yankees too. Carl Mays was showing the ball to the umpire, like there was something wrong with it.

I tried to get the security guard's hand off mine. He pulled me past the row where I had been sitting next to Ronnie.

"How did you know?" Ronnie asked, wide-eyed.

"I *told* you how I knew!" I yelled at him. "You should have listened! You could have helped me! We would have stopped it!"

"Shut up!" the security guard barked in my ear, pulling me up the steps.

A pinch runner was already on first base to take Chapman's place. Two doctors were out there now, holding a cup to Chapman's lips. He struggled to his feet once again, and the Yankee crowd gave him a polite round of applause. Ray took a few steps under his own power, and then he crumpled to the ground for good.

The crowd gasped again. Two guys ran out with a stretcher, but I couldn't see any more because the security guard was pulling me away.

I couldn't believe what was happening. They were just going to continue the game as if nothing unusual had happened. Nobody but me knew that Ray Chapman's beaning would be fatal.

"Get him to a hospital!" I repeated as the security guard dragged me away. "He's going to die!"

"I said shut up!" the security guard barked again.

He had just about pulled me down the steps leading to the bathrooms when that little jerk Ronnie came running over.

"Hey, kid!" he shouted.

"What do *you* want?" I asked.

"I just wanna know one thing. Are the Yanks gonna win the pennant this year?"

I looked at him, disgusted. "You think I'd tell *you*?"

Once we were out of sight of the rest of the fans, the security guard reached into his pocket and pulled out a set of handcuffs. I couldn't believe it when he yanked my arms behind my back and clicked the cuffs around my wrists.

"Is this really necessary?" I asked.

"I said *shut up*," he said, pulling me into the tunnel under the ballpark. "Let's go."

"Where are you taking me?" I asked.

"Someplace you can't bother nobody."

"Chapman's going to die!" I told him. "I can't believe you're wasting your time with me when there's a man who is dying out there."

"Kid, if you don't shut up, *you're* gonna be the one who's dying!"

"Am I going to go to jail?" I asked, as he dragged me through the tunnel.

"Maybe," he muttered, "if you're lucky."

We came to an unmarked door. He put a key into the lock, pulled the door open, and pushed me inside.

"After the game, the cops'll take care of you," he said. "And don't bother trying to get out of here. The door locks from the outside."

He slammed the door shut, and there was a loud click as he turned the key in the lock.

All I could think about was Ray Chapman. His skull was fractured, and those doctors didn't even know it. They were probably treating him with aspirin and Band-Aids. If it was the twenty-first century, somebody would have called 911 immediately. A helicopter would have been there in seconds to airlift him out of the Polo Grounds. He would be in a hospital by now, surrounded by doctors working desperately to save his life.

I looked around the room I had been locked in. There was nothing except one chair in the middle of the floor. A tiny window let in a little light. I could smell urine and alcohol. This must be where they put all the drunks and troublemakers, I figured.

I sat on the chair, disgusted. I should have knocked Mays out of the lineup when I had the chance. Or Chapman. There were so many things I should have done. But it was too late now.

I had blown it. Again. I didn't stop the Black Sox Scandal and save Shoeless Joe Jackson's career. I didn't help Jim Thorpe get back his Olympic medals. And now Ray Chapman was lying there dying. I always try to do the right thing, but it never seems to work out.

Look at me, I thought. Locked in a smelly room. Handcuffed. Who knows what will happen to me now?

Wait a minute.

I don't have to stay here! I have my baseball cards! I can just blow out of here and send myself home anytime I want! I don't even have to unlock the door. I'll just disappear. The police will never know what happened. They'll think I was like Houdini or something.

I went to reach for my baseball cards, but there was just one problem. They were in my front pocket. With my hands cuffed behind my back, I couldn't get to them. I struggled. It hurt my shoulder.

Some Houdini I am!

And then I remembered—the key! Houdini had given me that little key as a souvenir. He said it would open just about any lock in the world. It was in my back pocket!

I stood up and rooted around behind my back, trying to get the key. It wasn't in my left pocket; but when I reached into my right pocket, I found the little piece of metal.

Being very careful not to drop it, I took the key

in my right hand and scraped it over the handcuffs until I found the keyhole.

I was working blind, because I couldn't see what I was doing behind my back. The key fit, but it was a lot smaller than the hole. I pushed it around, jamming it against the lock mechanism every which way. Sweat was beading up on my forehead. I had no luck for five minutes or so, and then . . .

Click.

The cuffs opened and clattered to the floor.

Quickly, I reached into my front pocket and pulled out my new baseball cards. It didn't even matter which one. I grabbed one, sat down, and closed my eyes.

I just want to go home, I thought. I want to sleep in my own bed in my own house in my own time, where my mom would make me a bowl of oatmeal with brown sugar and everything would be fine again. I didn't need to save Ray Chapman, or anyone else. I just wanted to be safe.

And I didn't want to see a fastball coming at my head—or *anyone's* head—ever again.

After a few minutes, I started to feel the faintest tingling sensation in my fingertips.

The tingles got stronger and worked their way up my wrist. As they swept over my arm and across my chest, I knew that I was on my way home.

It all happened so fast. The next thing I knew, I felt myself slipping away.

15

Visitors

"YOU'RE GROUNDED, MISTER!"

Those were the first words out of my mother's mouth when she saw me in the kitchen getting something to eat.

"But, Mom—"

It was useless. It didn't matter what I said. She wasn't going to let me defend myself, anyway. I had never seen my mother so mad before.

"You were under strict orders not to leave this house," she told me. "I can't *believe* you would disobey me. Is this what it's like to have a teenager? You just ignore the rules? Do whatever you want to do? You had me worried sick! Where *were* you?"

"I was in 1920, trying to save Ray Chapman's life!" I said.

"I never even *heard* of that guy!" said my mother,

throwing her hands in the air. "What if something happened to you?"

There was no way I was going to tell my mom that something *did* happen to me. If she knew that a security guard had jumped me, handcuffed me, and locked me in a room, I would be grounded for *life*. She might say I could never travel through time again. Who knows? She might even take away my baseball card collection to make sure I didn't go anywhere.

Mom and I don't fight a lot. But this was one of those tense nights when neither of us wanted to talk to the other one and we tiptoed around the house trying to avoid seeing each other. I knew she would go to sleep without saying good night to me.

It must have been around nine o'clock that night when the doorbell rang. I was in my room flipping through a magazine. I got up to answer the door, but Mom beat me to it. By the time I got to the top of the stairs, Dr. Wright and Flip were standing in the front hallway.

"Is this a bad time?" asked the doctor.

"Not at all. Come in," said my mom. "Sorry about the mess. How about a cup of tea?"

"No, thank you, Mrs. Stoshack," Flip said. "We just had a bite to eat."

"Then what can I do for you?" Mom asked. "Is something wrong?"

I was in my pajamas but came down the steps, anyway.

"Your mother told me what you did today, Joseph," said Dr. Wright. "Are you okay? Any headaches? Dizziness? Vomiting?"

"No, I'm fine."

"Doc tells me you're good to go, Stosh," Flip said cheerfully. "You can play ball again."

"I've been thinking it over," I replied. "I'm not sure I want to play ball anymore."

"What?!" all three of them said at the same time.

"I won't ask you to pitch again," Flip said. "Promise. That was a dumb idea."

"It's not that," I explained. "I just . . . I don't want to play."

"But, Joey, you *love* baseball!" my mom protested.

"It's okay, Mrs. S. I've seen it a million times," Flip said. "He's a little gun-shy. It's natural after a guy gets hit. But you know what they say, Stosh. When you fall off a horse, you gotta get right back on."

"Horses don't throw 80 miles per hour," I said.

"Well, you take your time," Flip told me. "Whenever you're ready to come back, you're my starting shortstop."

"It was very kind of you to come over," my mom said, leading them to the door. "Very few doctors make house calls these days."

Dr. Wright stopped before they reached the door.

"There's something I'd like to ask Joseph," he said. "Would that be all right, Mrs. Stoshack?"

"Okay," Mom said, looking at me. I could tell she was still mad, but she had softened a bit.

"Joseph," the doctor said, "ever since Flip told me that story about Ray Chapman, I haven't been able to stop thinking about it. I've been obsessing about it, really."

"Wait a minute," Mom interrupted. "Who is this Ray Chapman guy I keep hearing about?"

"He was the only player in major-league baseball history to get hit by a ball and die," I explained. "He played for Cleveland. It was in 1920, before they had batting helmets."

"How terrible!" Mom said.

She went to the kitchen to get some chips and stuff while Dr. Wright and Flip sat on the couch. I pulled over a chair. The doctor took a newspaper article out of his jacket pocket and put it on the coffee table. Parts of it were highlighted in yellow. Mom came back with the snacks.

"I've been researching the tragedy. Chapman got hit right *here*," Dr. Wright said, touching his left temple. "The ball fractured his skull in the temporal lobe, which controls speech and language. But his brain was also injured on the opposite side, because a brain sort of bounces around inside the skull when the head is shaken severely. It's called a contra coup. I don't want to bore you with all the details—"

"No, go on," my mom said. "I'm interested."

I could tell that she wasn't just saying that to be polite. Mom's a nurse, and she's into all that blood-and-gore-and-guts stuff.

"Well, a blow to the head often causes blood

14 SPORTS

CHAPMAN SUFFERS SKULL FRACTURE

Cleveland Shortstop Victim of Severe Injury When Hit by Pitched Ball.

YANKS' RALLY FALLS SHORT

Hugmen Make Belated Attack in Ninth Inning, but Fail to Overtake Indians.

LEAGUE LEADERS WIN, 4 TO 3

Covelaskie and Mays Pitch Good Ball, but New York Boxman is Handicapped by Errors.

vessels in the brain to break," Dr. Wright continued. "This leads to what we call an epidural hematoma."

"Hema-what?" asked Flip.

"Hematoma," said Dr. Wright. "Blood builds up around the brain. The brain swells, and this puts intense pressure on the skull as delicate brain tissue is compressed."

"So what can surgeons do about it?" asked my mom.

"Well, we sometimes remove the cranial walls to give the brain room to swell or to drain the clotted blood," said Dr. Wright. "If necessary, we take out a good part of the skull; and after the swelling goes down and the brain has the chance to heal, we replace it with an acrylic implant."

"Ugh," Flip said. "Now you're grossin' me out."

"Actually, they knew about this in 1920," the doctor continued. "This article says they removed a small piece of Ray Chapman's skull, possibly to reduce the pressure. But the thing is, the surgery began after midnight. That was about eight hours after Chapman was hit. And that's the main reason why he died. Time is of the essence in these situations. The key is to quickly treat the secondary injury by controlling blood flow to the brain, blood pressure, and oxygenation. If you have a drop in blood flow, blood pressure, or blood sugar level, you're more likely to have severe brain damage."

"They probably didn't know all this in 1920," my mom said.

Dr. Wright nodded. "Nowadays, we know, for instance, that if one pupil is dilated, it means there's pressure on that side of the brain," Dr. Wright said. "If there's a skull fracture, we assume there's an epidural hematoma; and we operate right away. And we're much better at controlling bleeding and preventing infection. Even today, some patients with severe head trauma will die no matter what we do. But if they knew in 1920 what we know today, Ray Chapman probably would have survived. I'm confident of that."

"Okay," Mom said. "But what does any of this have to do with Joey?"

Flip had been pretty quiet this whole time. He put his hand on my mother's shoulder.

"That's why we came over tonight," Flip said. "Doc here wants Stosh to take him to 1920."

"I believe I can save Ray Chapman's life," said Dr. Wright.

16

The Deathball

I HAD TAKEN PEOPLE BACK IN TIME WITH ME BEFORE. FLIP came with me when I went back to 1942 to clock a Satchel Paige fastball. My mom came with me when I went back to 1863 to see if Abner Doubleday really invented baseball. So it wouldn't be a big deal to take Dr. Wright back with me to 1920. He couldn't do anything to stop that ball from hitting Ray Chapman's head. He couldn't run on the field and disrupt the game. But he might be able to perform an operation that would save Chapman's life.

Of course, if I was grounded, I wasn't going anywhere with anybody.

Flip, Dr. Wright, and I all turned to look at my mom.

"I don't know about this," she said. "When Joey took me back in time with him, we were nearly killed. What if something goes wrong this time? Or what if you save this Ray Chapman's life, and he becomes a criminal or something? What if he assassinates the president? Then Joey would be responsible."

I rolled my eyes. My mom is a bit of an assassination buff. She knows about every assassination in history.

"That's just crazy, Mom," I said. "Ray Chapman was a great guy. He wouldn't hurt anybody."

"On the other hand," Dr. Wright said, "what if we saved Ray Chapman's life, and he went on to discover a cure for cancer? Or what if he became the next Beethoven? You just never know."

Dr. Wright asked my mother if he could talk to her privately. They went to the kitchen. Flip and I were alone.

"Y'know, Stosh, we got a game on Friday," he told me.

"I saw the schedule," I said.

"We sure could use your glove at short."

"I don't think so, Flip," I said, avoiding his gaze. "I . . . I'm afraid."

"Not that I'm tryin' to pressure you or nothin'," Flip said. "But we haven't won since the day you got hit, Stosh. It would sure be a boost for the guys to see you out there on the field again."

Flip kept buttering me up, telling me what a good shortstop I am and how the kid who took my place chokes every time a ground ball is hit in his direction.

"I just don't know, Flip," I said, as Dr. Wright and my mom came back from the kitchen.

"I thought it over," Mom announced, as she sat down next to me. "You can go to 1920 if Dr. Wright is with you. You're officially ungrounded. But you better be careful!"

"All right!" Flip and Dr. Wright said, slapping hands.

"When should we go?" I asked Dr. Wright.

"The only day this week that I'm not on call is Thursday," said Dr. Wright. "Shall we say 6 P.M.?"

After school the next day I went to visit my dad. He knows a lot about baseball. It was my dad who first got me interested in baseball cards when I was little. He's the one who taught me how to play ball too.

That was before a drunk driver almost killed him. Dad is paralyzed from the waist down. He can't work and doesn't have a lot of money. But then, he didn't always work or have a lot of money before he got hurt either.

I wasn't really in the mood to visit my dad. I go see him once a week or so, mostly to make sure he's okay. We usually make popcorn and watch a game on TV. He lives in a handicapped-accessible apartment at the other end of Louisville. It has railings all over and one of those mechanical chairs that goes up and down the stairs.

"What's up, Joe!" he said cheerfully when I knocked on the door.

"Not much," I replied.

I never know if my dad really wants to know

what's up with me or if he's just making small talk. I didn't want to tell him that I was planning to go back to 1920 with Dr. Wright. He would be jealous. One time I took Dad back in time with me to see Babe Ruth, but that was before his accident.

"Wanna watch the Cubs game on the tube?" Dad asked.

"I guess."

"Dr. Wright told me you went and saw the Ray Chapman beaning," he said, as he tore the wrapper off a bag of microwave popcorn.

"Yeah. I tried to stop it, but I messed up."

"Terrible thing that happened to that guy," Dad said. "But then, who's to say which is worse, a blow to the head that kills you right away or not being able to move your legs for the rest of your life?"

Sometimes it's so depressing going to visit Dad. As the corn started to pop in the microwave, he took a soda out of the refrigerator for me and a beer for him.

"Listen," he continued, "Doc told me you're gonna try to save Chapman again. He's gonna operate on him or something?"

"Yeah, it's a long shot, I know."

"Well, sometimes long shots come in," he said, taking a swig of his beer. He lowered his voice to a whisper even though nobody else was around. "Listen, Joe, I was thinkin'. I got an idea that can make us some cash. A *lot* of cash."

I started to get a sick feeling in my stomach. Mom always says Dad should just get a steady job instead of wasting his time on lottery tickets and get-rich-quick schemes. Lots of handicapped people work. He's perfectly capable.

"Let's hear it," I said, not really wanting to.

"Okay," he said, "every serious fan knows that Chapman was the only player in history to get hit by a pitch and die. You were there. You saw it. Do you know what happened after that ball hit him?"

"It bounced back toward the pitcher," I said, remembering the scene in my head. "Carl Mays picked it up. He thought it hit Chapman's bat, so he threw it to first base."

"And what did the first baseman do with the ball?"

"I was looking at Chapman," I said, "but I guess the Yankees threw it around the infield and then back to Mays. Because a few seconds later, I saw him holding it and showing it to the umpire. It was all brown and dirty, because they used just one ball for the whole game. But I don't know what happened to it after that."

"That's right!" said my dad. "*Nobody* knows what happened to it after that. The ball was never recovered. You'd think it would be in the Baseball Hall of Fame or somethin'. But it's not. It was lost."

Dad just looked at me, a gleam in his eye. I didn't see what he was driving at.

But then I put two and two together.

"Are you asking me to go back to 1920 and get the ball that killed Ray Chapman?" I asked.

"Joe, do you have any idea how much that ball might be worth?" Dad asked excitedly. "Let me spell it out for you. M-I-L-L-I-O-N-S."

"Dad, that ball fractured Ray Chapman's skull," I said. "It killed him."

"Exactly my point," said my dad. "It's the death-ball. It's one of a kind. It might even have blood on it. Maybe you can get Mays to sign it. We could auction it off. It would be worth a fortune. Can you imagine what we could do with that money?"

"That's *sick*, Dad," I said. "How would you like it if the drunk who hit you autographed his car and auctioned it off?"

"It would be fine with me if we split it fifty-fifty," Dad replied.

I just shook my head sadly. I didn't want to hear it.

"Look, Joe," Dad continued, "if it wasn't for me, none of this time-traveling stuff would have happened, right? I'm the one who started you with baseball cards when you were little. I don't ask a lot in return. How about doin' me a favor?"

A few years back, I would have done it. Maybe I would have done it a few *weeks* back. I always did whatever my parents told me to do. That's how I was brought up.

"I'm sorry, Dad," I said. "I'd do just about anything for you. But not this."

I didn't stick around to watch the Cubs game. The popcorn was burned, anyway.

17

Makeover

AFTER SCHOOL ON THURSDAY, I RUSHED THROUGH MY homework. Then I rode my bike over to Flip's store to buy a fresh pack of baseball cards.

Mom and I didn't talk too much during dinner that night. I was a little nervous, like I always am before a trip. You never know what's going to happen. Maybe Dr. Wright would save Ray Chapman's life. Maybe he wouldn't. There was always the chance that something would go horribly wrong. There was the chance that I might not make it back home.

Mom went upstairs to read after she finished eating. While I was washing the dishes, there was a knock at the door. I went and looked through the peephole to make sure it was Dr. Wright. You've got to be careful who you open your door to these days.

There was a guy standing on the front porch. He

was dressed like a doctor, wearing one of those white coats; but it wasn't Dr. Wright.

It was a bald white guy. I figured that he was collecting for the local volunteer ambulance squad or something. My mom always gives them money, being a nurse and all.

I opened the door. The man was holding a black doctor's bag in one hand.

"Are you with the ambulance squad?" I asked.

"No," he replied. "I heard there was a boy in this neighborhood who has the unique ability to travel through time with baseball cards. I'm here to open up his brain and see what's wrong with him."

What?! This guy had to be putting me on. I leaned forward and looked at him closely.

"Who *are* you?" I asked.

"Joseph, it's me—Dr. Wright!" he said, laughing.

"But you're . . . white!"

"Of course I'm white!" Dr. Wright said. "Do you have any idea how long it took me to put on this makeup?"

"But why did you do that?" I asked.

"Joseph, do you really think they would let a black doctor perform brain surgery on a white man in 1920?" he asked. "Especially a *famous* white man?"

He had a point. I knew a lot about prejudice because I had already traveled back in time to meet Jackie Robinson and Satchel Paige. And that was in the 1940s. Prejudice against African-Americans was probably even worse in 1920.

"You shaved your head," I pointed out.

"Smooth, huh?" Dr. Wright said, touching his scalp. "I kinda like it. I just might keep it like this when we get back."

"Is Dr. Wright here, Joey?" Mom called from upstairs.

"No," I replied, "it's just some bald white guy."

My mother came downstairs; and when she saw Dr. Wright, she just cracked up. She ran to get her camera to take pictures.

"Oh, this is priceless!" Mom said, trying to hold the camera steady while she was giggling. "You're lighter than we are!"

After my mother finished snapping pictures, she went to get lunch bags for each of us; a fold-up umbrella; a first aid kit; and other silly, overprotective Mom stuff. While she was running around, Dr. Wright put his doctor bag on the coffee table.

"Will I be able to bring this along?" he asked. "I'm going to need it to perform the operation."

"Sure," I said. "What's in there, drills and saws and stuff?"

"No," Dr. Wright replied, zipping open the bag. "They pretty much had the tools they needed to cut through bone back in 1920. What they didn't have were our medications to reduce swelling, put the brain to sleep, and reduce the metabolism of the brain. I brought some barbiturates to induce a medical coma if necessary. And I'm bringing along a syringe, just in case. Oh, and a trephine, which is this tool we use to cut open the skull."

I really didn't want to hear all the details of how he was going to cut open Ray Chapman's skull. Just getting a blood test makes me feel woozy. I looked in Dr. Wright's bag and noticed there was a manila envelope in there too, like the kind they use in school.

"What's in the envelope?" I asked.

"Oh, that's my little secret," Dr. Wright replied.

Mom came in and put her stuff into Dr. Wright's bag. He zipped it shut.

"Do you have that new pack of cards you bought, Joey?" she asked.

"Yes, Mom," I said, patting my back pocket to be sure.

"Maybe you should put on some sunscreen," she suggested, "just in case."

"I'm *not* putting on sunscreen, Mom!"

I knew she would have liked to stick around, but she couldn't bear to watch me disappear. She told me to do everything Dr. Wright said, then hugged us both, kissed me on the forehead, told me to be careful, and went upstairs.

I sat on the couch, and Dr. Wright sat down next to me. He took a deep breath.

"Nervous?" I asked, turning off the light next to me.

"Yeah," he admitted. "I never did anything like this before. Will it hurt?"

"No," I told him. "It's sort of like going to sleep and waking up on a different planet."

It was strange to see Dr. Wright look so worried. Here was a guy who has opened up people's skulls and performed delicate surgery on their brains, but a little trip back to 1920 had given him the willies.

"Where will we end up?" he asked.

"I don't know exactly," I told him. "I usually land somewhere near the player on the card. But then I have to go find him."

"Do I need to do anything?"

"Just hold my hand," I said. "Close your eyes and relax. I'll do all the work."

I took his hand. It was sweaty. With my other hand, I picked up the Carl Mays card from the coffee table. I closed my eyes and thought about New York City. 1920. August.

It's funny how much you hear when you just stop talking and close your eyes. A car turned the corner around the block, and a plane flew overhead. The cicadas outside were chanting with the joy of being aboveground for the first time in 17 years. The house creaked.

After a minute or so, I felt the first stirrings of that tingling sensation in my fingertips that I had come to know so well. The buzzy feeling slid up my arm. I resisted the temptation to scratch it. Then it swept across my body to my other hand, which was holding Dr. Wright's.

"It's happening, isn't it?" I heard him mumble.

"Yeah," I whispered. "It's happening."

And then, we vanished.

18

Ruckus in the ER

WHEN I OPENED MY EYES, DR. WRIGHT AND I WERE standing outside a wooden door with a thin slot in it at about eye level. I turned around and immediately recognized where we were. It was the same area I'd landed the first time I went to 1920.

"Where are we?" Dr. Wright asked groggily.

"New York City," I replied. "Exactly where we need to be."

The sun was low in the sky. It had to be late afternoon. I knocked on the door, and the slot opened. A pair of eyes looked back at me.

"What's the password?" the man asked gruffly.

"Woodrow," I said, and the slot slid shut.

"How do you know the password?" asked Dr. Wright.

"I'm a regular here."

The door opened. The guy nodded to us and went

off somewhere. Behind him was a lady, and I recognized her right away. She was that nutty woman who'd introduced me to Babe Ruth. What was her name? Oh, yeah, Addie. Sweet Adeline.

"Stoshie!" she gushed, hugging me. "I thought you went to the Polo Grounds with Babe. Whatsa matter? Didja forget somethin'? Say, who's your handsome friend?"

"I *did* go to the game," I explained, "and then . . . I went home. And then I came back. Sort of. With my friend here, Dr. Wright."

"Hel-looo, Doctor!" Addie said. "You look like *Mr.* Right to me! I'd take some of *your* medicine any day."

"You're drunk," Dr. Wright said.

"And you're cute, sugar," she replied.

"What time is it?" I asked before things could get out of hand.

"Almost six," Addie said. "Where's the fire, for crying out loud? Why don't you boys come in for a while? Maybe the doc can give me a checkup from the neck up."

"Look," I told her, "this is gonna sound crazy, but this is an emergency. We came from the future. We live in the twenty-first century. You've got to believe me. We need your help."

"You say you're from the future?" she said, laughing, "And you think *I'm* drunk?"

"Forget about her, Joseph," Dr. Wright said. "The game started at three thirty. If it's six o'clock now, it already happened. Chapman has been hit. The game is over."

"Listen to me," I said to Addie. "A player on the Cleveland Indians is going to die. Dr. Wright is the only one who can save him. We need to get to the hospital right away."

"Which hospital?" she asked.

Huh! Good question. I didn't know which hospital they would bring Chapman to. It hadn't occurred to me that a city as big as New York probably had lots of hospitals.

"St. Lawrence Hospital!" said Dr. Wright.

"You boys are crazy," Addie said, "but I like you. Come on."

We followed her outside. It must have been rush hour, because the street was filled with lots of old-time cars zipping past, pumping out smoky exhaust. Dr. Wright put up his hand to hail a taxi, but none of them stopped.

"Here," Addie said, "let *me* do it."

She went to the curb, held up one hand in the air, and used the other to hike up her dress a few inches above her knee. A taxi immediately screeched to a halt.

"Get in!" she said, and the three of us piled into the backseat of the cab.

"457 West 163rd Street, and step on it!" Dr. Wright hollered to the driver. "St. Lawrence Hospital. It's about a half mile from the Polo Grounds."

"I like your style, Doc!" Addie said, as the cab

peeled away from the curb.

"How do you know which hospital to go to?" I asked Dr. Wright. "And where did you get the address?"

"I googled it," he replied.

"You *what*?" asked Addie.

"Never mind," he said. "I bet there's something on the news already about Ray Chapman getting beaned. Driver, can you turn on the radio, please?"

"Turn on the *what*?" the driver asked.

"Oh, forget it."

"These fellas come from the future," Addie said, giggling.

"I don't care *where* they come from," said the driver. "They better pay me in the present."

He was weaving in and out of traffic like a lunatic. The car had no seat belts, and the three of us were bouncing back and forth across the backseat like Ping-Pong balls. It wasn't long before we pulled up outside the hospital. Dr. Wright and I didn't have any money, so Addie gave the driver some coins. We jumped out of the cab and ran to the front entrance.

"Perhaps you two should wait out here," Dr. Wright said, his hand on the door.

"Nothin' doin'," said Addie. "I got you here. I'm comin' in."

"That goes double for me," I said.

"All right," Dr. Wright said, "but just . . . be cool."

"Why?" Addie asked. "It's hot out."

We rushed over to the reception desk. There was

a woman sitting there wearing old-lady glasses. She looked up at us pleasantly.

"Excuse me, ma'am," said Dr. Wright, "can you please tell me which room Ray Chapman is in?"

"The baseball player?" she said. "They wheeled him into the emergency room about 15 minutes ago. Poor fellow. But, Doctor, these people with you won't be allowed—"

"Let's go!" Dr. Wright barked.

We followed the EMERGENCY ROOM signs, running down the zigzag hallways behind Dr. Wright. I was completely out of breath. Finally, he pushed through the door that opened into the waiting area of the emergency room.

It was a somber scene in there. A bunch of the Indians, still in their baseball uniforms, were gathered in small groups, whispering to each other. Their arms were on each other's shoulders.

I recognized Tris Speaker in the corner. He was trying to console a sobbing woman with light brown hair. She looked like she was in her twenties, and she looked like she might be pregnant. I thought I recognized her from the photo in Ray Chapman's locker. It had to be his wife.

"Ray's gonna die!" she moaned, her head on Speaker's shoulder. "I just know he's gonna die!"

"Not if I can help it!" announced Dr. Wright.

Everyone in the emergency room turned and looked at him. Dr. Wright rushed over to the nurse behind the desk.

"Do you work here?" she asked.

"I'm Dr. Louis Wright. I must see Ray Chapman right away!"

"Please take a seat," the nurse told him. "As soon as his doctor is available, I'll ask him to step in and speak with you. He is currently examining the patient, trying to determine the best course of action."

"The best course of action is to perform surgery *immediately*!" Dr. Wright thundered. "That man is going to die unless I am allowed to operate right away!"

The nurse rolled her eyes, like she was sick of dealing with doctors.

"I'll see what I can do," she said.

I was afraid that Dr. Wright might just bust down the door, but a doctor came out right at that moment. He had a stethoscope around his neck and a name tag that read DR. KOLANDER.

"What's going on out here?" he demanded.

"I'm Ray Chapman's personal physician," Dr. Wright lied. "I'm visiting from Cleveland, and I know exactly what happened. I must examine Mr. Chapman immediately."

"Um-hmm," said Dr. Kolander. "And who is this young lady?"

"She's our friend," I volunteered.

"Quiet, Stosh," said Dr. Wright.

"Charmed," Addie said, extending her hand gracefully. "The name is Adeline. Like the song. But *you* can call me Addie."

"Do you always bring kids and floozies with you when you examine patients, Doctor?" sneered Dr. Kolander.

"Hey, I ain't no floozy!" yelled Addie, and she slapped the doctor in the face. He rubbed his cheek for a moment before continuing.

"Mr. Chapman is going to be fine," Dr. Kolander said slowly. "We are examining him very carefully, and we will make the decision whether or not to operate in a few hours. So if you folks will just be patient—"

"Look," Dr. Wright said, getting into the other doctor's face, "Ray Chapman's skull is fractured! He has an epidural hematoma. Do you even know what that means? His brain is swelling as we speak! If we don't relieve the pressure on his brain right away, he's going to die no matter what else you do!"

"You certainly know a lot about this patient," Dr. Kolander said, "considering that you haven't examined him since the injury."

"I didn't want to get into this," Dr. Wright said, "but I guess I have to. This boy and I come from the future. We live in the twenty-first century. Medical science will advance dramatically in the next hundred years. I know some things you couldn't possibly even dream about. I have researched this case. I can save Ray Chapman's life, if you will just give me the chance."

Dr. Kolander looked at me, then at Dr. Wright, unimpressed.

"Why are you sweating, Doctor?" asked Dr. Kolander.

"We rushed over here," I volunteered.

Dr. Kolander took a handkerchief out of his pocket and wiped it across the top of Dr. Wright's forehead. A line of dark skin appeared.

"Just as I suspected," Dr. Kolander said. "You're a Negro posing as a white man! Nurse, please call security."

"That's it," Addie said as she ran for the door. "I'm outta here! I can't afford to be arrested again."

Dr. Wright wiped some of the makeup off his face with his sleeve.

"The color of my skin is irrelevant!" he yelled. "Do you want to save Chapman's life or not? His brain has been injured on both sides. There is a rupture of the middle meningeal artery. We need to put in a fiber optic pressure monitor; and we need to control blood flow to the brain, blood pressure, and oxygenation. I have medicine in my bag that will reduce the swelling and metabolism of his brain. He needs a hemicraniectomy. I can do that. You can't. Are you going to assist me, or are you just going to stand there like a fool?"

Dr. Kolander stood there for a moment, like a fool.

"You're delusional," he said. Then he yelled, "Security! We have an insane colored man and a boy in the emergency room."

The door flew open. But it wasn't a security guard.

It was a guy in a Yankees uniform.

"Who are *you*?" asked Dr. Kolander.

"That's Carl Mays!" I said.

All the Indians who had been standing around watching the argument turned and glared at Mays.

"What are *you* doing here?" asked Tris Speaker.

"Is Chapman okay?" Mays asked. "I feel terrible about what happened. If he dies, I'm gonna quit baseball."

"You shoulda quit yesterday," one of the Indians said. "It's too late now."

"This isn't a good place for you, Mays," said Tris Speaker. "Not now."

At that moment, the door flew open again, and two security guards rushed in with nightsticks.

"What's the problem, Dr. Kolander?" asked one of them.

"These two men are causing a ruckus," he replied.

"You're wasting valuable time!" shouted Dr. Wright as he unzipped his black bag and started taking out things. "Here, I'll prove it to you. This is a medicine that will essentially put the brain to sleep. And this is a trephine. It's a tool we use to cut open the skull."

"It's a knife!" yelled the nurse. "He's got a knife!"

"Take them away!" Dr. Kolander said to the security guards. "Put them in the insane ward!"

One of the security guards grabbed Dr. Wright from behind, and the other one grabbed me. He held the nightstick against my neck and yanked my arm behind my back.

"Let's go, sonny," he grunted.

As he dragged me away, I saw Dr. Wright reach into his bag and pull out that manila envelope he had put in there. He tossed it to Dr. Kolander.

19

The Future

I COULDN'T BELIEVE WHAT WAS HAPPENING. A GUY WITH arms that were thicker than my legs had wrapped a straitjacket around me and tied it tight. Then he picked me up, hoisted me over his shoulder, and carried me down the hallway.

"Dr. Wright!" I shouted.

"Shut yer trap!" barked the goon who was carrying me. "Before it fills with flies."

He carried me down the winding hall until he passed a sign that said INSANE WARD. Then he pulled open an unmarked door and dumped me on the floor.

"See you in the next century!" he said with a snort. He slammed the heavy door behind him as he left.

Not *again*!

I looked around. This time it wasn't a room. It was more like a cell. Dank. Dark. No furniture. No nothing.

A minute later the door opened, startling me. The goon was back. This time he was carrying Dr. Wright over his shoulder. He threw him down roughly.

"I brought you some company," he said to me, "in case you get lonely. Ha-ha-ha-ha!"

He left, slamming the door. A key clicked in the lock.

Dr. Wright stood up and leaned his shoulder against the wall.

"Padded cell," he said. "Nice."

"Why did they put us in here?" I asked.

"So we can't smash our heads against the wall and try to kill ourselves," he replied.

"People really do that?"

"Sure," Dr. Wright told me, "if they're frustrated enough."

"But this is a *hospital*," I said. "They're supposed to make people *better*."

"Mental illness wasn't understood very well a century ago," said Dr. Wright. "They didn't know what to do with insane people. So they locked them up, like criminals."

"We're not insane!" I said.

"They *think* we are," Dr. Wright said. "And who can blame them? We said we came from the future. A crazy black man wearing makeup was telling them how to perform brain surgery. No wonder they thought we were nuts."

I had to laugh. And I realized that our situation wasn't actually as desperate as it appeared. All we had to do was get the pack of new baseball cards out of my back pocket. We could use one to blow out of there and go back to our own time.

The only problem was that my hands were wrapped tightly. I couldn't move them. We positioned ourselves back-to-back so Dr. Wright could try to get at my back pocket. But his straitjacket was longer than mine, and he could barely get his fingertips out. He turned around and tried to untie my straitjacket with his teeth.

"Hurry up!" I said as he struggled. "Somebody could come in at any second!"

"I . . . can't . . . do it," Dr. Wright said, grunting from the effort. He was sweating. Finally, he tumbled to the floor, exhausted. He lay there for a minute, panting.

It finally sunk in. We could be stuck here. Somebody would eventually find my baseball cards and take them away. There would be no way to get back to our time. We would have to live our lives starting in 1920 . . . in an insane asylum.

I did the math in my head. If I was 13 years old in 1920, I'd be 93 in 2000. Hardly anybody lives that long. What was the life expectancy in 1920, anyway? Probably 60 or so.

I wouldn't live to see the millennium. I wouldn't live long enough to see my own birth.

I wish I had listened to my mom all the times she'd warned me about the dangers of time traveling. Now I would never see her again.

My chest tightened. Tears were welling up in my eyes.

"It's my fault," I choked.

"No," Dr. Wright said. "I'm the adult. I should have anticipated all the possibilities."

It didn't matter whose fault it was. We were stuck in 1920, and we were going to die sometime in the twentieth century. Nobody from our time would ever know what happened to us.

Maybe I could write a note, I thought. I would write a note to my parents and tell them how much I loved them. I'd find a way to make sure the note got to them in the future. I could take it to Louisville and hide it in the house where I would grow up and—

No, that was crazy. They might get the note before I was born. It wouldn't mean anything to them. Or the previous owner of the house might find my note and throw it away.

Wait a minute. My house wasn't *built* in 1920. There was no place to hide a note for my parents to find.

I sat down and leaned against the wall next to Dr. Wright. My eyes were watery, and my shoulders were heaving. I didn't even try to pretend that I wasn't crying. I just let it out. I couldn't even wipe the tears off my face.

Dr. Wright leaned against me and told me everything would work out. We'd find a way out of here, he insisted. He was just trying to make me feel better.

We were both quiet for a few minutes. I was trying to resign myself to my fate.

"If we get out of this," Dr. Wright finally said, "what will you do when you get home?"

"Hug my mom," I said right away.

"No, I mean, with your life?" he asked.

"I don't know," I replied. "Something I never did before. Maybe learn how to play guitar. Drums, maybe."

"What about baseball?" he asked.

"I've been playing ball for a long time," I said. "The kids are getting bigger and stronger, throwing and hitting the ball harder. A lot of guys are giving up baseball."

"Coach Valentini told me you're one of the best players on the team," Dr. Wright said.

"Not good enough to get out of the way if a ball is coming at me," I replied.

"Look, Joseph, bad things happen in life sometimes," Dr. Wright said. "That was a fluke. You can't just avoid things every time something bad happens to you. When I was in med school, we had this patient who got hurt in a traffic accident, so she decided not to drive anymore. Fair enough. Then she had a bad experience at a supermarket, and she decided not to go grocery shopping anymore. Eventually, she just sat inside all the time. She figured she would never have a bad experience that way. And she didn't. She never had *any* experiences."

"I have nightmares about getting hit again," I

confided. "That ball came at me so fast. I never even saw it."

Dr. Wright struggled to his feet and went over to examine the padded wall.

"You know, I almost quit medicine right after I finished school," he said, as he looked to see if there was a crack or another door somewhere along the wall.

"What happened?" I asked.

"I was performing an endoscopic pituitary procedure on a man," Dr. Wright told me. "He was one of my first patients. I did the operation correctly, just the way I was taught. But the guy died, anyway. Sometimes, no matter what we do, the patient still dies. I was aware of that possibility. But I was devastated."

"Why didn't you quit?" I asked.

"I thought about it," Dr. Wright said. "I could have gone to law school, or studied business or something else. But I knew that wouldn't make me happy. I love medicine. I love the idea of taking a sick person and making them better. If you do what you love, you'll love what you do."

I thought about what he said for a few minutes, then asked him the same question he asked me.

"If we get out of this, what will *you* do when you get home?"

"Me? I'm hoping to travel to the future."

"Huh?"

"Joseph, do you remember that envelope I brought with me?" Dr. Wright asked.

"Yeah," I said. "What was in there?"

"Before we left home," he said excitedly, "I wrote out the proper way to do an epidural hematoma. I explained why the surgery needs to be done as soon as they find a skull fracture in a patient. I also wrote all I knew about penicillin; the polio vaccine; the dangers of cholesterol, trans fats, cigarette smoking, and AIDS. I told them about seat belts, air bags, and CAT scans. I told them about all the advances in the health care field that have taken place in the last 90 years."

"Them?" I asked. "Who's them?"

"The doctors of 1920," Dr. Wright said. "You see, Joseph, I've always wondered what would have happened if the lightbulb, for instance, or the airplane had been invented a hundred years earlier. Technology would have moved along a century faster. It would almost be like traveling to the future."

"I don't quite get it," I admitted.

"Joseph, if I can travel back in time and give the doctors of the past something they don't yet have, or teach them something they don't yet know, I can essentially push time and medicine forward."

"So when you return to your own time, everything would be more advanced than it was when you left?" I asked. "Because the people living in the past had a century to use what you told them?"

"Exactly!" said Dr. Wright. "I didn't come with you to 1920 just to save Ray Chapman, Joseph. I came here to save *thousands* of people. Maybe millions. I gave the envelope to that doctor. If he reads what I wrote and publishes that information, it will be a different world when we get home. Medical science will have advanced nearly a century."

"What do you think will change?" I asked.

"Each of us is born with a certain number of nerve cells. We don't grow new ones, and we gradually lose the ones we have. The holy grail for doctors like me is to regenerate nerve cells, to figure out how to create new ones. We could cure so many diseases, and help so many people. If I could be around to see that—well, it would be my way of traveling to the future."

I always thought it would be cool to travel to the future too. They'll probably have flying cars and microwave freezers, stuff like that. But I would need a future baseball card, of course. And they're not printed yet. So traveling to the future is pretty much impossible.

It was interesting to think about, but none of that stuff mattered. We were stuck in 1920. Dr. Wright couldn't find any cracks in the wall. The door was sealed shut. We weren't going to the future. We weren't going to the past. We weren't going *anywhere*.

"Man, you'd have to be a Houdini to get out of this place," Dr. Wright mumbled.

I stopped.

"What did you just say?" I asked.

"I said you'd have to be a Houdini to get out of here."

Yeah, Houdini. *He* would be able to get out. He could escape from *anything*.

That's when I figured it out.

"I know how we can do it!" I told Dr. Wright.

"How?"

"When I got hit by that ball," I said, "I fell down and dislocated my shoulder."

"So?"

"So when I came to 1920 the first time, I saw Houdini escape from a straitjacket while he was hanging upside down outside a building," I said excitedly. "Later, in that bar we went to, he told me how he did it. His trick for escaping from a straitjacket was to dislocate his shoulder!"

"What?!" Dr. Wright said. "That's crazy."

"Houdini told me that when your shoulder is dislocated once, it is easier to dislocate it again."

"Well, that's true," said Dr. Wright. "The ligaments become slightly lax. You're not actually planning to dislocate your shoulder, are you?"

I wasn't waiting around for anybody's permission. I moved my shoulder up and down, forward and back. There wasn't much give inside the straitjacket, but there was a little. I closed my eyes, gritted my teeth, and rolled my shoulder around in its socket.

"Careful, Joseph."

It hurt. It hurt bad. Whenever I moved my shoulder forward, a bolt of pain shot through my upper body. Sweat was dripping off my nose.

"You don't have to do this, Joseph," said Dr.

Wright. "We'll find another way out of here."

"And what if we don't?" I yelled at him.

I forced my shoulder forward, fighting the pain. Sweat was pouring off my forehead. I was reaching the threshold of how much pain I could bear.

"Stop it, Joseph! I'm afraid you're going to permanently damage—"

"I'm not quitting!" I said. "You didn't quit!"

I strained just a bit further. And then I felt a pop.

"I did it!" I grunted.

The pain was so intense I could barely breathe. But with my shoulder out of its socket, there was just a little extra room in the straitjacket. The pain was unbearable, but I wriggled around until I could feel the straps start to loosen. I jumped up and down, trying to get gravity to do some of the work. I must have *really* looked like a crazy person.

Little by little I was able to get one strap loose. Dr. Wright pulled at it with his teeth. I had some breathing room now. The other straps were starting to slacken. I wriggled and twisted and spun around, trying to get them off.

Finally, the straps fell away. I ripped off the straitjacket with my good hand and flung it aside.

"I'm Houdini!" I exclaimed.

I started untying Dr. Wright's straitjacket. It wasn't easy with just one good hand, but I did it. Dr. Wright finished the job and tossed his straitjacket against the wall. Then he grabbed me by the shoulder.

"You're going to feel a little pressure, Joseph," he

said. Before I knew what was happening, he pulled on my shoulder hard.

Craaackkkk.

"Owwwww!" I yelled, as my shoulder popped back into place.

"Okay!" Dr. Wright said. "Get one of your baseball cards! Let's get out of here!"

I found the cards in my pocket and quickly ripped open the pack. It felt warm. I grabbed a random card in one hand and held Dr. Wright's hand with the other.

We closed our eyes. I thought about going home. To Louisville. In *our* time.

In the distance, I heard what sounded like footsteps coming down the hallway.

"Hurry, Joseph!" urged Dr. Wright. "I think they're coming."

I concentrated on the card in my hand; and after what seemed like an eternity, the tingling sensation arrived on my fingertips.

The footsteps were getting louder.

The vibrating feeling moved up my hand, up my arm, and across my chest.

"Something's happening!"

The footsteps stopped outside the door.

My whole body was vibrating now. I had reached the point of no return. My entire body was buzzing.

There was the sound of a key in the lock.

I almost felt like my body was rising up, floating over itself, and spinning around.

The door squeaked open. I resisted the temptation to open my eyes.

"Hey, what's goin' on in here?!" somebody yelled.

"So long, sucker," Dr. Wright mumbled.

And then we disappeared.

20

The Decision

DR. WRIGHT AND I TUMBLED INTO MY LIVING ROOM HEAD over heels, crashing into the coffee table and knocking over a floor lamp. My mother was standing there with the vacuum cleaner.

"What happened to *you* guys?" she asked.

Dr. Wright and I looked at each other. We were a sweaty, disheveled mess. A lot of Dr. Wright's makeup had been rubbed off, so part of his face was white and part was black.

"It's a long story, Mom," I replied.

"I hope nothing bad happened."

Dr. Wright and I looked at each other again.

"Not really," he said, getting up and brushing off his pants. "Joseph is a very . . . *resourceful* young man."

"It was really an educational trip, Mom," I said before he could give her any details.

I always tell my mom that stuff is educational. If she thinks I'm learning something, she doesn't give me such a hard time about it. But if she knew that I was straitjacketed and thrown into a padded cell in an insane ward, and that I'd intentionally dislocated my shoulder to avoid being stuck in 1920, she'd never let me travel through time again. It's better for her to think the whole experience was like a field trip to a living history museum.

"So, were you able to save that baseball player's life?" my mother asked.

"No," Dr. Wright said, "that didn't quite work out as we had planned."

"Mom," I said, "did anything change while we were away?"

"Change?" she asked. "Like what?"

"Like, do you have a flying car now? Or a microwave freezer? Anything like that?"

"Well, sure!" Mom said. "Doesn't everybody? I was just going to fly over to the supermarket now to pick up some liquified ice cream. Want to come?"

"You're kidding, right?" I asked.

"Of course I'm kidding!" she replied. "Flying cars? Joey, are you out of your mind?"

"Let me ask you this, Mrs. Stoshack," said Dr. Wright. "Is everything the same over at the hospital? Have there been any major medical advances in the brief time we were in 1920? Techniques for regenerating nerve cells? Or for treating head injuries, perhaps? Anything like that?"

"Not that I know of," my mother said. "Everything is pretty much the same. I'm sorry."

Dr. Wright's shoulders fell. He sat down on the couch with a sigh. I sat next to him.

"We tried our best," I told him. "That's what counts, right? I guess that doctor didn't open your envelope."

"Or maybe he just didn't believe that what I wrote could possibly be true," he said sadly. "If some strange doctor showed up at *my* hospital and told me what was going to happen in the next hundred years, I guess I would think he was crazy too."

"I don't know *what* you guys are talking about," my mother said.

The phone rang, and she ran to the kitchen to answer it. Dr. Wright told me he should be heading home. He got up and shook my hand.

"Thanks for taking me with you," he said. "Even if we didn't save any lives, it was an experience I will never forget."

"No problem," I said. "Thanks for taking care of me at the hospital."

"Joey!" my mom called. "It's Coach Valentini. He wants to speak to you."

I went to the kitchen and took the phone.

"Stosh," Flip said, "I just wanted to remind you we got a game today, and it starts in an hour. You don't have to play if you don't want to, but I wanted to make sure you knew about it."

"I . . . I don't know," I said into the phone.

"It's okay," Flip said. "I understand. It's up to you. But you're our shortstop if you want it."

Dr. Wright was saying good-bye to my mom at the front door. I thought about some of the things he told me when we were locked up in that padded cell. I thought about how he almost quit medicine after one of his first patients died. I thought about the lady who never left her house. And I came to a decision.

"I'll *be* there," I told Flip.

I hung up the phone and went to change into my uniform.

Facts and Fictions

Everything in this book is true, except for the stuff I made up. It's only fair to tell you which is which.

The true stuff: Houdini really did live in New York in 1920, eat needles, and escape from a strait-jacket while hanging upside down. Whether or not he was able to dislocate his shoulder on purpose is a matter of debate.

Prohibition really did start a few months before this story takes place. At one point, there were more than 30,000 illegal saloons in New York City.

Women really did win the right to vote the day after Ray Chapman died, when Tennessee ratified the 19th Amendment to the Constitution.

Babe Ruth and Carl Mays really did not get along and almost fought on several occasions. Most of the baseball stuff is true and can be found in Mike Sowell's great book *The Pitch That Killed: The Story of*

Carl Mays, Ray Chapman, and the Pennant Race of 1920. Read it. I also learned a lot from old copies of *The New York Times* and *Baseball's Great Tragedy: The Story of Carl Mays* by Bob McGarigle.

What happened to the Cleveland Indians?

After Ray Chapman was hit, the Indians went on to win the game. Cleveland kept a slight lead in the standings on the White Sox and the Yankees.

But after Chapman's death, the Indians lost seven of their next nine games. The White Sox (eight of whom would soon be banned from baseball for throwing the previous World Series) opened up a three-game lead. It looked like Cleveland might collapse.

But they didn't. Dedicating the season to their fallen shortstop, the Indians went on a rampage and won the American League pennant, then went on to win the 1920 World Series too. They only won it one other time, in 1948.

What happened to Ray Chapman?

The doctors waited until after midnight to operate on Chapman. He died four hours later.

Thousands of people attended the funeral in Cleveland, and thousands more couldn't fit into the church. Players on both teams attended but not Chapman's close friend and manager, Tris Speaker. He had collapsed and suffered a nervous breakdown.

CLEVELAND (A.)	Ab	R	H	Po	A
Jamieson,lf	5	0	2	1	0
Chapman,ss	1	0	0	0	3
Lunte,ss	1	0	0	0	2
Speaker,cf	4	1	0	0	0
Smith,rf	4	0	0	2	0
Gardner,3b	3	1	1	2	1
O'Neill,c	4	2	3	8	0
Johnston,1b	4	0	1	10	1
W'gans,2b	4	0	0	4	2
Coveleskie,p	3	0	0	0	3
Total....	33	4	7	27	12

NEW YORK (A.)	Ab	R	H	Po	A
Ward,3b	4	0	0	1	0
P'k'p'gh,ss	4	0	0	3	1
Ruth,rf	4	1	1	1	0
Pratt,2b	3	1	1	1	4
Lewis,lf	4	0	0	0	0
Pipp,1b	3	0	0	12	0
Bodie,cf	4	1	2	4	0
Ruel,o	3	0	2	5	1
Mays,p	2	0	0	0	4
aVick	1	0	1	0	0
Thormalen,p	0	0	0	0	1
bOdoul	1	0	0	0	0
Total....	33	3	7	27	11

a Batted for Mays in eighth inning.
b Batted for Thormahlen in ninth inning.
Errors—Ward, Ruel.

Cleveland .... 0 1 0 2 1 0 0 0 0—4
New York .... 0 0 0 0 0 0 0 0 3—3

Two-base hit—Bodie. Home run—O'Neill. Sacrifices — Chapman, Ruel, Coveleskie. Double play—Pipp (unassisted). Left on bases—Cleveland 6, New York 6. Bases on balls—Off Mays 1, Coveleskie 2. Hits—Off Mays, 7 in 8 innings; Thormahlen, 0 in 1. Hit by pitcher—By Mays (Chapman). Struck out—By Mays 3, Coveleskie 4. Losing pitcher—Mays. Umpires—Messrs. Connolly and Nallin. Time of game, one hour and fifty-five minutes.

The fatal game.

Ray Chapman is buried in Lake View Cemetery in Cleveland.

The ball that hit him is not necessarily missing. The Sports Immortals Museum in Boca Raton, Florida, claims to have it.

Ray's wife, Kathleen, was not actually at the hospital right after the accident. She got the news in Cleveland and didn't arrive in New York until the next morning, after Ray had died. She was three months pregnant at the time; and a daughter, Rae Marie Chapman, was born on February 27, 1921.

After Ray died, Kathleen never attended another baseball game; and in 1928, she took her own life. A year later, Rae died from measles. She was only eight years old.

What happened to Carl Mays?

After Ray Chapman died, Carl Mays was the most hated man in baseball. Mostly, it was his own fault. Instead of being remorseful (as he appears in Chapter 18), he blamed others for the tragedy. He claimed there was a scuff mark on the ball and the umpire should have thrown it out of the game. He said Chapman ducked into the pitch. Mays did *not* show up at the hospital after the accident and (upon the advice of the Yankee management) didn't attend Chapman's funeral either.

Mays faced a strong reaction, from MAYS THE MURDERER being scrawled in locker rooms to opposing players yelling "Murderer!" from their dugouts when he was on the field. He received death threats. Many American League teams threatened to boycott games unless Mays was kicked out of baseball.

It never happened. There was also talk of banning underhand pitching. One change that *did* come was that umpires began to throw out balls that were scuffed or dirty. That, and the success of Babe Ruth, ushered in the home run era.

Baseball also began experimenting with batting helmets after the Chapman tragedy. But they would not become mandatory until the late 1950s.

Ray Chapman was only the fifth batter Carl Mays hit in 1920, and the only one he hit in the head. While he was known as a "headhunter," Mays hit only 89 batters in his career. Walter Johnson hit 203—the most by any pitcher. For the record, Cy Young hit 163, and Nolan Ryan hit 158.

Carl Mays did not actually consider quitting baseball after Chapman died. In fact, he pitched a shutout in his next game and won his next four in a row. He finished the season with a record of 26-11 and continued his very successful (208-126) career. He grew bitter when pitchers with similar records, like Rube Marquard (201-177) and Stan Coveleski (215-142), were inducted into the Baseball Hall of Fame.

Here's a trivia question for you. Who was the second Yankee (after Babe Ruth) to hit a homer in Yankee Stadium? It was Carl Mays. He was also the last pitcher to clinch a world championship for the Red Sox in the twentieth century.

After he retired, Carl Mays went home to Oregon, where he was a scout for several teams and ran a baseball camp. He lost his life savings in the 1929 stock market crash. His wife died at age 36 from an eye infection. They had two young children.

For fifty years, Carl Mays had to live with the fact that he had killed a man. "Nobody ever remembers me for anything except that one pitch," he used to say.

He was right. When he died in 1971, the obituaries focused almost entirely on what happened to Ray Chapman.

Carl Mays is buried in River View Cemetery in Portland, Oregon.

Louis T. Wright is the name of a pioneering African-American surgeon who was born in 1891 (the same year as Chapman and Mays). I learned of Louis Wright from Howard Camerik's novel *The Curse of Carl Mays*.

Stosh, his mom, and Flip are fictional characters. So is Adeline, but that *is* my mom's name, and this book is dedicated to her.

THE NEW YORK TIMES, TUESDAY, APRIL 6, 1971

Carl Mays, Yankee Whose Pitch Killed Batter in 1920, Is Dead

SAN DIEGO, April 5 (AP)—Carl Mays, the New York Yankees pitcher who threw the fastball that hit and killed Cleveland batter Ray Chapman in 1920, died yesterday in El Cajon Valley Hospital. He was 79 years old.

Mays, who won 208 games as a hurler for four major league clubs, was later a scout for 20 years.

The right-hander, whose specialty was the submarine pitch, shook off the effects of Chapman's death to finish the 1920 season with 26 victories. He steadfastly maintained that Chapman, a right-handed hitting shortstop, lunged out of the batter's box in the game at the Polo Grounds in which he was hit.

The following year Mays posted a 27-9 record for the Yankees, his career high.

In 1924 he was traded to the Cincinnati Reds and posted 20 wins against 9 losses. He was 19-12 with the Reds in 1926. His over-all earned run average of 2.92 ranked him 14th among all-time pitchers.

Before he joined the Yankees, Mays won both games of a double-header against Philadelphia to clinch the pennant for Boston in 1918.

As a Yankee he pitched in the first game in Yankee Stadium (opened April 18, 1923) and was a roommate of Babe Ruth.

He finished his playing career with the New York Giants but remained in baseball as a scout for Milwaukee and Cleveland.

International

Carl Mays as a Yankee

Surviving are his widow, Esther; a son, Carl Jr., and a daughter, Mrs. Betty Barker.

Photo Credits

This author would like to acknowledge the following for use of photographs: Nina Wallace: 16, 48. Library of Congress: 25, 62, 70. National Baseball Hall of Fame Library, Cooperstown, NY: 32, 67, 79, 87, 96, 99.

About the Author

This is Dan Gutman's ninth Baseball Card Adventure. If you like it, check out *Honus & Me, Jackie & Me, Babe & Me, Shoeless Joe & Me, Mickey & Me, Abner & Me, Satch & Me,* and *Jim & Me*. Dan (seen here at Ray Chapman's grave) is also the author of *The Kid Who Ran for President, The Homework Machine, The Million Dollar Shot, Johnny Hangtime*, and the My Weird School series. You can find out more about Dan and his books at www.dangutman.com.

Sam Gutman

Be sure to read each

BASEBALL CARD ADVENTURE

in the home-run series!

Travel through time with Stosh to meet the greatest baseball players in history!

HARPER
An Imprint of HarperCollins*Publishers*

www.harpercollinschildrens.com

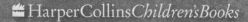